Midwest Literary Journal

Volume 2

Fall / Winter 2021

This Literary Journal contains writings by members of the Midwest Writers Guild of Evansville, Indiana.

Midwest Writers Guild Literary Journal: Volume 2 Fall/Winter 2021

Midwest Writers Guild of Evansville © 2022
Copyright © Midwest Writers Guild of Evansville, Indiana
All rights reserved.

ISBN: 978-1-937668-06-8

Graphic Design by John William McMullen & Whitney Arvin
Edited by Tim Heerdink
Published by Bird Brain Publishing

Bird Brain Publishing is an imprint of Bird Brain Productions.
www.birdbrainpublishing.com

All reprint rights are reserved except with permission from the authors, as stipulated under the U.S. Copyright of 1976.

No part of this book shall be reproduced or transmitted in any form or by any means, electronic, mechanical, magnetic, photographic (including photocopying), recording or by any information storage or retrieval system without prior permission of the authors. No patent liability is assumed with respect to the use of the information contained herein. Although every precaution has been taken in the preparation of this book, the publisher and authors resume no responsibility for errors or omissions. Neither is any liability assumed for damages resulting from the use of the information contained herein.

Summary: The Fall/Winter 2021 Anthology of Short Stories, Essays, and Poems by Members of the Midwest Writers Guild of Evansville, Indiana

ISBN: 978-1-937668-06-8

Paperback

Printed in the United States of America

Midwest Writers Guild of Evansville

2021 Officers

President: Tim Heerdink

Vice President: Jake Harris

Treasurer: Don Brooks

Secretary: Wendy Eastman

Membership in the guild is open to anyone of any age who is interested in writing, whether experienced or novice. As a guild, our goal is to help each other develop writing skills and learn what it takes to see our writing goals realized.

The guild meets the second Tuesday of every month at Your Brother's Bookstore at 6:30 p.m. in Evansville, Indiana.

Table of Contents

Contest Winners

First Place:	Feast/Safe	Jake dh	1
Second Place:	The Final War	Don Brooks	9
Third Place:	Just Let it Go	Shannon McKinney	27

Short Stories   29

Liturgy of the Forsaken	John William McMullen	31
Unearthing	Joshua Britton	37
The Finding of Estelle	M. Dianne Berry	49
Aunt Salomie's Revenge	Phil Kline	57
The Misfits of Seventh Grade	Wendy Eastman	61

Poetry

My Black Dahlia Poison Caterpillar	David L. O'Nan	75
Sensible Shoes	Erin Pennington	76
You, Before	Jerrica Magill	77
Life on Venus	Jerrica Magill	78
I Still Forgive	Jerrica Magill	79
Emerald Peaks on My Mind	Jerrica Magill	80

Senseless	M. Dianne Berry	81
Sea of Trees	M. Grace Bernardin	83
The Voice	M. Grace Bernardin	85
The Third Option (Paralyzed)	M. Grace Bernardin	86
My One Last Dream	M. Grace Bernardin	88
Woods	M. Grace Bernardin	90
The Light I Can't Avoid	M. Grace Bernardin	92
Beautiful Memory	M. Grace Bernardin	93
Walls Fall Down	Richard Westbrook	95
Taking the Trip back to Innocence	Tim Heerdink	96
Wishes for My Last Birthday with You	Tim Heerdink	98
Harmacy	Tim Heerdink	100
Meal of Memory	Tim Heerdink	102
Breach	Tim Heerdink	103

Reviews

Review for *The Ghosts of Our Words Will be Heroes in Hell* by The NÜ PROFITS OF P/O/E/T/I/C DI$CHORD
Tim Heerdink   107

Contest Winners

First Place

Feast/Safe

by Jake dh

    The cold silver shimmer of a distant full moon shines deeply inside a desolate forest. A gust of wind gently blows through these Midwestern woods, nestled in Southern Indiana. No human should be around for several miles.
    This fact did not escape the bipedal beast quickly making its way through the slightly illuminated forest. Two yellow eyes pierced the darkness from over seven feet off of the ground. The dominant part of its mind only focused on one singular urge.
    Feast.
    It needed to feed more than anything, not necessarily for sustenance; the person that it used to be had eaten relatively recently. The transformation into beast didn't use bodily energy in the most common sense of the word. The forces that enacted the curse of the wolf didn't correspond to natural rules. And neither did this all-consuming hunger.
    Feed. Devour. So hungry. Must... feast!
    The creature relentlessly ripped its way toward where people should be. Animal prey would work in a pinch, but human flesh and blood really quenched its savage urges. Taking human life into itself defined the curse that transfigured the former human. When the night ended and the moon fell from the sky, the curse would end. The wolf knew it. The person buried deep inside barraging predatory instinct knew it. That's why she transformed

into this thing so far from civilization. She swore never to never take another innocent life ever again.

The human laid down in the corner of this monster's mind as it fruitlessly attempted to seek out mortal prey. She attempted to give it false ideas. Steer it just slightly away from people. She worried that the beast might be moving at such a high velocity that it might be able to beat the clock and kill again.

A peaceful dirt road that had occasional traffic this time of night resided a few miles to the west. In the mind of the wolf, the woman could only see the outside world through the equivalent of a pinhole, and thus remained the slight level of her influence over the beast. She could still use that slight influence to keep it running away from that road. Next time the change came, she would go even deeper into the woods. Even having potential cars this close to her made her nervous. Luckily, the scent of exhaust didn't register as prey to the monster she had become trapped inside.

The room the human woman resided in felt claustrophobic. Small and compact. She felt as if she might suffocate at any moment. Over the last few years, she came to understand that very few things could possibly kill her in this inhuman form. She knew her temporary discomfort would fade.

A different scent entered the nostrils of the wolf. The creature laid its massive four digit hand on a nearby tree. The massive lupinoid raised its wet nose into the night air to get a better whiff. The woman on the inside could smell it, too. She saw a vision of an outline. A small bipedal... no, not any type of animal, but seemed too small, too young to be an adult.

Easy prey. Easy meal. Feast!

The beast's 'thoughts' filled the woman's mind. She could hear that killer instinct as if it were a jet engine revving up next to her head.

No. Run the opposite direction. There's so much juicy prey in the other direction.

The woman tried to use her small amount of influence to redirect the ravenous werewolf back into the woods. She felt drool dripping from its starving jaws. Her lie didn't seem to have much of an effect.

Must have my fill. Chewing and grinding...

The woman peeked through the pinhole in her mind's eye.

Thick, salty blood.

A small beam of moonlight shone from the small opening.

Gooey, stringy flesh. So little time. So much hunger.

She observed the beast's rampage across the woods. Soil and wooden splinters thrown into the air as it hurled toward its next meal.

Splintered, crunchy bones...

The woman made out a small figure in the distance. The small being hunched over supporting its weight against a nearby tree. Staring into the small opening in her mind reminded her of how little influence she wielded in this instance. If the ever closer growing silhouette were what she thought it was; she could only look away at the horror that would inevitably unfold. The atrocity her body would commit against her clear and defined will.

A tiny whimper echoed in the woman's ears. The small, high pitched crying bounced off of the walls in this room that didn't actually exist. A room her psyche created in order for her to keep ahold a thread of her sanity. The woman inside of the beast understood that this monster that took control of her under the light of the full moon intended to murder this person. She wondered how this small child found herself in this forest in the middle of the night.

The hungry wolf couldn't have been further than a dozen yards from its prey. The woman's mind became consumed with panic.

I can't live with this. Not again. Not this time. Think, Caroline, think!

Caroline closed her eyes tight to avoid the bloody death about to unfold in front of her. "NO!" she screamed with every ounce of emotion and willpower. With everything that she was. Every ounce of what made her... human.

She felt the momentum of the monster halt. She didn't taste blood in her mouth or hear the death cries of a young girl. The woman opened her 'eyes' in mind space where she existed in this moment. The small pinhole that she viewed the world through, that she exerted her hopelessly small amount of influence over the wolf had become larger. Much larger. The room had also widened to resemble an apartment that also doubled as an office. Almost exactly like the one she used in her day to day life, but normally the window didn't spew moonlight into her home. Buildings in the city typically block this much natural light from shining through.

A window. A real window allowed Caroline to see the real world. Not only did the pinhole grow to such a large size in her moment of desperation, her influence over the wolf seemed to be much stronger.

She clearly saw the little girl, eight or nine years old, shivering and terrified. The wolf's eyes grew soft and no longer bared its teeth. The woman wrested some amount of control from the creature on the outside.

Why? How? Need to move. Need to kill small tasty...

No. Not this time. She's scared, but...

The wolf opened its hand exposing the palm of its massive paw/hand. The girl sniffled back tears, but laid her tiny glove in the middle of the monster's palm. A metal cling swung back and forth from the bottom of her wrist. Handcuffs linked her two tiny arms together. Red marks adorned her tiny wrists. Blood... small amounts of blood stained her coat.

...she's not afraid of us.

Caroline racked her brain, trying to compartmentalize information so the wolf didn't see everything. She needed to take the girl within a half of a mile or so of the roads. Then try to steer the monster away while the girl runs in the opposite direction. Someone should pick her up within an hour or so.

We need to take her in this direction. I need to make sure she's safe.

The wolf's body stopped in midstride. The little girl seemed confused. "Are you going to help me, Miss Wolf?"

A surprised look adorned Caroline's face, most humans didn't catch her wolf's gender correctly.

Very observant.

I need to feed. Stop making me do things.

Caroline felt teeth exposing themselves to the girl. She knew that she didn't have complete control of the situation.

I'll let you feed on the next person we come across. I promise. Just not her. Just this one time. Please.

Promise?

"Hey, girlie!" A masculine voice emanated from behind the wolf. "I only snatched you from that park yesterday. Come on, I brought you out here for fun, and we didn't have any fun yet..." The disgusting sack of refuse posing as a man stopped dead in his tracks, locking eyes with a creature that easily cleared seven feet tall.

Feast?!

Given that this man had outed his intentions, what he really was, this decision quickly came to Caroline.

Absolutely.

"What in the hell is that?!" The man's flashlight illuminated the monstrous creature.

The woman inside let the beast take over. Its insatiable hunger lunged to consume every ounce of the "man" in front of them.

The kidnapper raised the hand opposite of his flashlight hand. Neither the wolf nor the person in its mind noticed the snub-nosed revolver until the half-second before it fired straight into the large werewolf's left eye. This stunned the creature.

Caroline stood aghast as a cascade of blood drenched half of her apartment window. A red geyser erupted from the wound, pouring all over the soil. Caroline felt her apartment shake as the creature struggled to push through the pain. It attempted to find its footing as the prey ran deeper into the forest.

Both entities in the same body felt the stinging pain, as both knew that this wound would not kill them, only slow them down. Anything other than silver only prolonged the inevitable bloody death coming for that molesting garbage. The wolf and Caroline heard the same thing. Two sets of footsteps sprinting away from the injured creature. The little girl... and her pursuer bounding after her. The extent of his mental illness showed through the fact that even though he just came face to face with this lumbering supernatural monster, that the man still chased after his own prey.

The two became one. Focused on one single goal. The dismemberment of that wretched predator. Killing the real monster. The werewolf didn't merely dash through the forest after the two, but they ripped their way through the brush. Splinters and debris scattered into the air. This made the wolf give off a sort of wake or shockwave as it burst into a clearing.

The man took a deep breath as he observed the little girl still trying to escape his grasp. This seemed to be a useless endeavor given that he was much bigger and much faster. "Not sure if that thing is dead." He huffed and puffed. The child predator knew that he couldn't take any chances. This girl had seen his face. Any decent police sketch artist could identify him. "Can't have any loose ends." He stared down the chrome revolver straight into the little girl's face. "Such a waste."

The little girl scrambled to push her way through the loose soil in order to avoid the gunshot coming her way. This guy shot a werewolf in the face, she understood, even at her age, that she didn't have much of a chance to avoid this shot.

Both the girl and the man heard a heavy thud slamming against the dirt in the direction whence they fled. The man span around to take aim at that monster again, but this time its speed overtook him. The joint between his hand and arm became disconnected within seconds. Blood spurted on the dismembered hand still futilely grasping the handgun as if it still offered any protection.

The molester turned to flee, grasping his gushing stub. Long razors sunk their way into the soft flesh of his shoulder, holding him in place. Dropping him to his knees. The monster's eyes didn't reflect savagery or hunger in this moment. Only purpose. Both the werewolf and the dying man faced the little girl as she stood frozen in shock.

The large grey fur covered hand raised with one single digit extended. It motioned in the direction slightly to the left of the girl. The little girl understood, seeing the softness in the creature's eyes. She knew that this werewolf indeed wanted to help her.

As the girl skittered into the darkness, the dual minded monster focused back on the task at hand.

You used your claws. That means if he survives the night, he'll be like us. We can't have that. End it.

The massive left hand of the wolf closed around the face of the screaming man in front of them, muffling the terrified pleas for help... for mercy coming from his despicable maw.

No problems.

Gargantuan jaws crunched down on the tender flesh of its victim's neck. Gurgling death echoed through the darkness.

Two dozen police officers scoured the forest. They followed instructions given to them by the little girl who had been picked up on the country road about three quarters of a mile from this location. It took an hour for her to flag down a car, but she got to safety.

The officers didn't believe her outlandish story about a grey werewolf saving her, but occasional wolf sightings did happen here and there. They kept the focus of their investigation on the kidnapping. To see if they could indeed find the sack of shit that grabbed her from a park thirty miles away.

One officer began to heave at the sight of something brutally sickening. The next officer kept her composure, but she understood why her fellow police officer spilled his guts on the forest ground. If this was indeed the person they were looking for, it might be quite the challenge to identify his mutilated corpse.

She had seen animal attacks before, but this seemed to be the worst she'd ever encountered. The man's collarbone had been split on the right side of his neck. The inside of his chest cavity had been chewed away from that opening. Much of his flesh from the rest of his appendages had been gnawed on as well. The look of terror had been frozen on the half of his face that still had skin on it.

On a hill relatively far away, Caroline peeked her head out from behind a large tree. She smiled as she observed the army of law enforcement casing the forest. She seemed comfortable, despite not wearing any clothes. She'd become accustomed to waking up like this. Nude in the great outdoors.

"Good. That means she's safe." The woman breathed a literal sigh of relief. She reached into her mind's eye. *Are you still hungry, big girl?*

No. No more feasting. Sleepy.

Great, because the next full moon is like in twenty-eight days. I need to go deeper into the woods next time. Or figure out something better than... this.

She sprinted into the woods to avoid being captured by the police. She's always been a free spirit at heart. Even before all of this.

Second Place

The Final War

by Don Brooks

"I write this inscription in haste, knowing my time is ever nearer; I write this seeing unusual signs in the cosmos that are in a state of imbalance; I write this with hope the contents of this capsule will lend itself to an explanation in a better place and time should opportunity once again return.

To my dearest friends, I must tell you what I have seen and of things to come.

We live on a planet we are not capable of leaving, and although we have technologies far greater than has ever been known to mankind, and recognize there are thousands of places throughout our galaxy and many solar systems, yet we see no place hospitable to our species.

We can see lightyears away but no way to examine, let alone go there as conditions on earth deteriorate. Many places on earth have become massive waste pits to deposit our refuse, where life can no longer be sustained, in such regions, and each year enlarged by hundreds of square kilometers, it accounts for over two percent of our planet's landmass. The combined wastelands, extensive lagoons, lay oozing gases, bubbling pocks, producing strains of streptococcal, pathogens, and virally infested vermin that feed on fluids from the colossal cesspits. Many of the pools are hundreds of square kilometers totaling an area one-half of the landmass encompassing the District of Australia.

The year is 2254, the month, Augustus, and the day, the 10th. My name is Lawrence Heathcliff. My position is Adjutant Commander in service to the *World Management Centre* Police.

178 years earlier, Manhattan was in the city of New York, in the District of North America. It was ceded to the United Nations, which today is referred to as the World Management Centre.

Harlem and East Rivers border it on the east and the Hudson River on the west. It administers the world's previous 195 countries, today reorganized, it is the planet government seat for its 19 world districts.

All of Canada, to the Mexican border, is currently District Three. We live here.

The *Re-Org Wars*, from 2078 through 2110, took the lives of 1.3 billion, leaving the planet with its 19 districts and a population of 8.3 billion, easing care somewhat for the remaining inhabitants.

In the early years of the 21st century, philosophers saw the first of two groups pulling frantically at the fabric of humankind. In simple terms, two forces identified the equity and quality of life. One, Ethnos, was comparable to the social order springing up in the formative years of America's United States, the virtuous years. This period brought an era like none other before. However, even then, charlatans existed, and certainly still do, yet today, their numbers are hundreds of percentages higher.

Common in the country's formative years, and among the masses, was a study of persons with depraved or evil behavior by psychologists. Since that time, arguments about them have ensued, seeking to locate evil.

From within our finite minds, it seems truly not serious or a condition that is frequent enough to warrant much attention. Nevertheless, it is a condition of which we need to be cognizant.

However, before considering a study, someone would have to first care! Moreover, this is precisely where the matter died.

Was it a serious matter, we would think to pursue it? Should it not bring anguish into your life, you nor others would care. However, it does bring anguish to many, and too often.

We must name it although few wish to. Where did 'evil' have its beginning? Certainly, it was several millennia ago, but where or even more so, how did it come to be?

Over subsequent centuries, seditious groups, ill-intended, sprang up as movements, most without a name, and as if by some common spirit, to eradicate virtuous principles moving the United States of America from its foundational premise. When once good people began to move from their roots into a pseudo-alliance with evil, a fall became destined.

Media of past centuries always informed bilaterally. Commonly, there were no shades of gray and very little prejudice. In the passing of time and the cost of goods inched upward, just as the cost of 'truth,' does, so truth became available to the highest bidder or the greater of power players.

Like many, that practice double-speak, misleading as many as will listen, which is most, and carrying poison away to be consumed by others. The obverse is all that stands between the longevity of 'we the people' and desolation.

War need not be seen to exist. We can commonly see the evidence, the carnage.

These two forces are moving headlong toward one another; only one will have its way. And only one will remain.

Returning to the future and the *Re-Org Wars,* the wars, mostly small, were propagated on a premise of melding contiguous countries to reduce conflicts and ease the planet's crowdedness.

The word freedom had outlived its usefulness in these times. A managerial system could meet the needs of the smaller, the ill-informed, and impoverished countries, but still all the more - tightly governed and better controlled by a central power in the earth.

Indeed, many changes have occurred. One unforeseen matter was the human life span, a double-edged sword.

The human life span has increased to 115 years for women and 104 for men. The political unrest, however, left an incredible number, unimpressed with the quality of life in comparison to earlier years. Of such human lineage, I come. I was birthed in 2132, of an Ethnos heritage, and by necessity, closeted, as you will come to understand. In this capacity, I have served 37 years as Secretary of State. The history that was available reflected on early years what had been referred to by some, my age, as *'Golden Years'* before technology had fully come, the period prior to 2078.

Today, people cannot imagine a time when society lived in individual dwellings. Living now in tall modular skyscrapers is so much more efficient.

Most amenities are now provided with one monthly amount, which includes dietary needs, medical attention, and all of it withdrawn from one's employment stipend. Today, no longer is euthanasia a matter of concern. It is a neat and painless procedure.

Today, a government payment schedule dictates the amount paid to a family upon termination. Abortion is a free service for the full term and with an L&D (live or die) option available for defective bodies following birth.

The present Secretary-General of the United Nations is Alexandrea Lebedev, whose home of origin is District 17, or the former Russian block. She began her term one year ago, with nine years remaining.

To attain the position, she devoted her first thirty years to education, the next ten to government servitude, and finally was elected as deputy secretary, the first from her district, then followed by a general election of the combined districts, she became Secretary-General. Not to be confused, only deputy secretaries or higher-ranking dignitaries from each district may vote. It assured that only the most excellent candidates could participate.

Our planet has proven too small for its estimated 23,543,000,000 occupants. In the year, 2160 colonization of the moon began. Mars was next to be considered.

Over the passing centuries, society needed to be modified. Humanity, with the gift of ingenious minds, continued with work-a-rounds at every hand.

Prior to 2078, our world struggled with behavioral issues. 2078 issued in new, exciting but not health-giving changes.

1.
For thousands of years, we were only able to experiment with the culture to curb the seeming naturally recurring nature of hurting one another. In addition, for hundreds of years, society attempted to develop a human strain without criminal natures.

2.
Volumes of work were compiled in an attempt to scour evil from humankind. It was always unsuccessful. It was a perplexing condition that could not be eradicated.

3.
Numbers of sects have always sought interventions, struggling to change themselves and others.

4.
Philosophers and psychologists alike looked at the various strains of human behavior, in hopes of unlocking the secrets of hostility toward others. Seemingly, it is impossible to do interventions to curb those who openly were in opposition to goodness, kindness, and caring for others.

5.
Yet, often without apparent reason, opposition to the research continued to exist. It is as if, within our DNA, a subordinate battle rages of which we seemingly have no knowledge. In

each situation, it resides in 'good virtues versus bad' or 'good virtue over evil.' It was as if good and bad had no relativity, no form in which to coexist. An ancient position concerning goods and services, as well as the behavior toward others, once again returned. It was that of 'caveat venditor' that the seller is responsible for any problem that the buyer might encounter with a product or service.

There has never been a period when tension or fear has not been present within us. Yet, my beloved fellow traveler, I have received insight; the time of imminent urgency is upon us. We are about to feel the Hand of wrath fall.

Often viewpoints resulting in injuries to others persist. Compromise is how we try to move forward if we cannot find common ground. However, compromise does not necessarily mean peace. A compromise was thought to be the spirit of a win-win that was foundational in the framing of many nations' guiding principles.

Harmony became highly sought after all because it elicits peace. We all wanted peace, security from danger, and unrest. Lives full of unrest bring threats and risks.

In addition, we discover some take extreme measures to achieve personal gain. Others give a great deal, so some may enjoy pleasure with no lack of comfort and peace.

With peace, seldom seen are those who will not relent from attaining their ambition by force of their perspective upon others using deceit or any imaginable form of coercion. Many cannot conceive to do otherwise is possible. However, more than ever, it has become the rule and not the exception.

Those who would deprive us of life to achieve harmful social conditions are there not to sustain life but to eradicate it; it is they who will not preserve humanity but overcome through double-speak and lies to overwhelm the common people. The common evil!

They consider it nothing to crawl over the bodies of their dead and wounded to proselyte just one good man or woman, to crush or annihilate that single voice of reason.

Occasionally, earth sees such decadence. Who is this unnamed army? Who is their captain? Yet, they are there, each day, bombarding others, attempting to overthrow rational thinking people. We see them. We hear them. However, we cannot understand them.

We ask, 'How can such a venomous ilk exist?' Never stopping, always persisting, ever-present, they wear down the common person.

Each year becomes less rational than the previous. Does civilization become a castaway in time? Are we to become as cultures from antiquity, unlearned, and without a contribution?

Therefore, it is; concerns with degrees or levels of contention shared by all, and to all by varying degrees. It is not agreeable, but the opposite has never been known to achieve it, although humankind has in ways tried to change it.

Nevertheless, as hope springs eternal, so with the young, especially, we reattempt it from their idealism, to correct it or recreate reason only to find weariness eventually wearing them down, and so all reach the same place, despair.

It stems from something from within our emotional DNA. It is not taught. It is an emotion from somewhere within, a deep and unknown source that lies within us. As age ascends, idealism wains and disappears; thus, when nothing changes, - nothing changes. Moreover, sooner or later, we discover it is not within us to change the pattern of creation, and we come to accept it, turning us into the problem as well.

We know chaos is wrong, yet doing whatever is generally needed to extend survival, we do, while infecting the emotional core of those younger, prompting them to come to terms with what we have discovered as reality.

There is an opposite, or opposing group, whose design it is to appeal to our baser nature; it pretends to hold a line of civility, against all odds, against all hostilities, and all contentions. It is within this setting; our elucidation can become an agent for change.

Of our beginning, we cannot speak clearly. We can say that as humanity began to create records, we can somewhat see our history.

At first blush, we discover patterns, repetitions that of the establishment of nature in the ebb and flow of time. More commonly, it has been said, not knowing history, we, therefore, are doomed to repeat it to our detriment.

No doubt, the first step forward toward truism and integrity, must be found for students of our time, to return to our roots, recommit to principles for good, moving out, an army to restore our land.

Next, we need to call the enemy by its name, corrupt and debased, incorrigible, and denying them platforms from which to endanger our young and all of us in general.

Along the time continuum, 1776 was a monumental moment for those who were Americans, with the spirit of colonists, commonly sensed as the exuberance felt in youth, full of optimism and hope.

Nevertheless, how long does the endangered and oppressed, labor under the degenerate ploys perpetrated upon a people by evil?

Apart from the people came a voice of one, loudly crying out, "You cannot withstand me. Each passing century you are losing position."

The voice was that of Apollyon, the archenemy of Theotes.

Apollyon was from a long time past. Some say of him, likely millions of earth years ago. A flaw within him grew increasingly diabolic with time. His gaze would bring certain death.

It was told he could look upon an object and it would shrivel, turning to a greenish vapor and disappear in moments. It was he who was credited with all debauchery, war, and death.

The evidence of 'Apollyon's' wrath was surmounting, with each century as the hearts of humankind became more darkened.

It was not that mayhem was not present from the first day, but when multiplied millions of people of light were cast out and trampled on, there was no concern whatsoever. People of light refer to those who know the path of goodness and, as best they can, by so trying, endeavor to walk in the light.

Contrariwise, people of darkness are dangerous people.

Early Apollyon, given an opening, was offered an opportunity to have a little time; he seized it in the hope of the annihilation of all. Annihilation as in the complete and utter disappearance of creation. The time was short, however, enough that through the centuries, he had burgeoned it many times over.

Theotes made no response. None was needed. His words were true and final.

Therefore, the battle began. Humanness was given to know it could choose. Apollyon's crafty intellect was far greater than humanness of mortals and soon overcame with simple baiting, with poison bait, the bait of 'pride.' With this infusion of bizarre intellect and capability of infecting and incapacitating the will of all, truth has died.

Having acquired the knowledge needed to be evil, it seems possible it was something inbred and highly likely to be perpetrated on others, as needed.

Evil has its own network.

Those who subdue it and live controlling it do not have receivers as it were to hear or respond to it.

It is as if they cannot hear the broadcast of malevolence. Their minds can't hear or entertain the thoughts broadcast by the beast. They become numb and poisoned. Such is simply not the thinking of the Ethnos.

Most often, within minutes of meeting someone, we see supporting evidence that provides clues. Pursuing an inquiry, we learn quickly if this person is one of our own.

Alexandrea Lebedev was a follower of Apollyon. As was the case with most, she did not know it. It hasn't only to do with appearance but with the default of the intellect.

Just as in the early 21st century, when media was infected. Today, the year 2254, media is a department of the present UN, and what they approve is published and circulated.

It was coined in the early 21st century; they were called out as 'fake news.' Upon the earth today, there are pockets of dissenters, but in such numbers, they no longer pose a threat. It wasn't so much Lebedev needed to be a follower; she already was and didn't know it, which is why she rose through the ranks.

Again, there seems to be a general frequency, as we understand radio signals, a kind of spiritual or ethereal signal the majority of such minds are attuned.

Similarly, and oddly enough, evil minds recognize one another without codes, passwords, or cognizant recognition. It might be through speech, practices, or body language. No one knew how or why, yet it is never discussed. Each species affiliates with its kind, be it physical or political. Alternatively, other comparisons will work, as well. It is true also, persons without evil or even differing levels of goodwill associate with their own kind, with either those who are unsoiled or those who are soiled.

It is early familial indicators that set the frequency of a minor's mind. It is thought likely, but just impossible to say with any certainty.

Since 2110, few conflicts have broken out. Throughout the ensuing eighty-one years, there have been only two. Each had occurred over land grab issues. In District Ten, the territory of South Sudan tried to take several hundreds of acres from Ethiopia.

There were many injuries but no loss of life. The UN was praised with quelling the uprising in large part by the earlier confiscation of all guns from the earth. As of 2191, no weapons are manufactured except for those of the United Nations police.

All confiscated weapons have been melted and the steel used for infrastructure, as needed. One nation at a time, they were stripped of their firearms beginning in 2115.

The last, District Three, was the former countries of Canada and the United States. That conflict lasted eighteen months and took 22,537 lives. An additional 2,340 UN police died.

The UN celebrated with the rest of the world. A world at peace, for the first time ever.

Yet, unreported homicide numbers are the highest in recorded history. Guns were all that was reported on. In no way did it stop the killing, maiming, and thievery. That had increased by alarming numbers. Now, it was knives, axes, and an assortment of many unusual objects. The most unusual was the case of the murder of a young man by the father of an eight-year-old girl, in District Four. The father used the dry jawbone of a donkey. The teeth had left bloody contusions all over the young man's body, including his skull. The girl recovered.

A new pattern began to follow. Be it night or day, gangs, mostly the young, roamed, intimidating, and taking what goods they wished without resistance. The business of locking one's home grew five-fold in only the first year following the confiscation of weapons. Penalties enacted for minor crimes were more severe but without effect.

Any bodily injury or death in the commission of a crime was punishable by death and was adjudicated within 30 days of the crime.

Nevertheless, publicly celebrated, was that at last, 'peace and safety' was boasted of around the globe, including the lunar colony. All the centuries past, all the bloodshed, and all the continual tension that had been broadcast in government-run media concerning crime, now disappeared, not to be heard again. Man, himself, had mastered order and discipline.

No mention was made of Apollyon as none considered he even coexisted with man. Man had prospered on his own. There was no power but man. No other existed.

One last thing considered and desired to bring utopia to earth was the means to extend life for those who chose to. A few smirked as they observed; it was the living - who were ultimately in favor of perpetual life. Those euthanized certainly had no vote!
Even as the joy was enveloping the earth, the earth was groaning. Its sound had not reached the people.
Theotes was moving. Was there to be a day of reckoning to come soon? Were opposites about to engage? He was known to be slow to anger and slow to wrath. When he spoke, he commonly whispered.
Apollyon, full of pride and with much time passed, had forgotten the words of Theotes. He had forgotten Theotes.
First, to come and virtually unnoticed, weather patterns began to change. Casually reported was that earth was warming. Deserts commonly reaching 54 degrees Celsius, were now frequently recording temperatures of 69 degrees.
Experts were quick to point out the lack of care during the 17th, 18th, and 19th centuries as the primary causation. The greatest influences pointed to were greenhouse gases, carbon dioxide, methane, fossil fuels that had been burned over hundreds of years. Also, during those industrial years, deforestation compounded the problem by reducing the needed oxygen.
Unnoticed oceanic coastal areas rose by six-and-a-half centimeters last year – an unalarming change considered by many.
Solar power had come into its own but not enough or soon enough. It and wind power were not produced in enough quantity, until the end of the 21st century.
Moreover, although greenhouse gases slowed, it had not been reduced enough nor soon enough to avoid rolling blackouts occasionally.

It was a hardship, but the UN would fix it in time. After all, the new age had mastered all things presented to it.

Then, eight months following, during the night in District Seven, formerly Chile, slid from the base of the Andes Mountains, off the coast from Antofagasta, northward, to the border of Peru, a result of a massive wall of underwater earthquakes. The tsunami following in many places reversed and splashed backward over the National Flamencos Reserve up to 2,768 meters of height.

The United Nations met in an emergency session. The estimate was 1.2 billion loss of lives. The injured were minimal by comparison. It was likened to a surgical cut of 680 square kilometers of the countries nearly 800,000 square kilometers, simply just washed into the sea.

Two months later, when the Mount of Olives experienced an earthquake, superstitious humankind was thrown into world panic. The earthquake had split it from east to west, causing some small sects to believe an apocalyptic prophecy had occurred. The United Nations quickly addressed the geological activity, and the direction of the five-mile-long fissure was geologically explained satisfactorily.

It displaced 4,567 families, killing 3,245, and injuring a number that couldn't be tabulated. District One sustained the loss, and Mohamed Ashkan, a closeted Ethnos and Deputy Minister was going head-to-head with Alexandrea Lebedev concerning needed help in the district.

Funds had been denied because the loss sustained was somewhat less than the amount required to trigger UN assistance.

He would call for a vote of no confidence at Session in the coming meeting in 55 days. Although the difference in dollars was miniscule, Mohamed felt they must have financial help.

World support was strong for Ashkan. Should the UN Council not censure Lebedev, it could lead to a vote to unseat her.

Twenty-three days before the Manhattan Council, Ashkan died in his Gian speeder. Following an investigation, it was determined to be an intentional act, using an LGL (light generated laser), having melted the vehicle with him as its sole occupant. He was a compatriot of mine and is sorely missed.

Five days before the meeting, Lebedev was found in her bath closet, poisoned. Her assistant Secretary-General was appointed and sworn in at the Manhattan Council. Here-in is my confession; I was a coconspirator to her demise. She was a wicked person. UN funds did go to District One.

Unusual and cataclysmic events began on the planet. Unannounced, significant solar flares bombarded earth, blacking out one district and then another.

The moon, commonly moving from its orbit an inch a year, became erratic. Its orbit reduced by 122 centimeters last year caused hundreds of tsunamis over the Pacific Ocean's Ring of Fire. Similar occurrences happened in the Atlantic. Tides some places rose by more than two-and-a-half meters.

Concern was pandemic about the earth as each district braced itself. Large numbers of people were missing from around the globe. It was thought the masses could have gone to seemingly safe places. It seemed few to none knew where such places were.

Ten months following the Pacific tides, the moon once more began moving from the earth as its gravity fell to 1.60 m/s². Seas calmed worldwide. Surfing was no longer a viable sport, as most seas lay flat and smooth.

Greater darkness was increasing but slowly. Exponentially, though, it increased with each day. As the moon increased its orbit radius, the stability of the earth decreased, causing a greater wobble at its poles. More severe weather patterns developed; for the first time, reported heavy snows accumulated in the southern borders of District Three.

From 2245 through 2247, District 12 was pelted with thousands of asteroids ranging from very small to the largest measuring 0.627 kilometers in diameter. Its greatest concentration was in the former states of Russia and China. The earth was darkened for fourteen months. Estimates of death were from six to eight million.

The National Oceanic and Atmospheric Administration realized there was an increase of distant space material moving to the many black holes of space, disappearing, such as TON $M_\odot$ an ultra-massive black hole, with an extremely luminous quasar located near the North Galactic Pole in the constellation Canes Venatici. Vladimir Creshenko, the newly elected Secretary-General, was informed of the activity, reacting in shock and dismay, he notified all districts of the impending collapse.

Sensing the conclusion of such matters, I hurried to find a cylinder of Tungsten, measuring three centimeters in diameter and thirty centimeters in length, a capsule for this document, in hopes of preserving information for another people. Finishing it, I placed my name and signature on it, including the date, Augustus, the 23rd day, 1430 hours, the year of 2254. I sealed it, placing it in my personal repository with little hope of preservation."

Epilogue

It was the following day in my compartment; I collapsed to the floor in a trance-like stupor. Fully aware of myself and surroundings, I moved away from my body, watching all as if in a dream-like state.

The earth's moon had turned to dust blown past the earth's atmosphere and by solar winds, disappearing as though it never existed.

Space debris near the earth fell as molten junk, flaming out before impact. Message transmission disappeared as gamma rays possibly absorbed signal. By now, no life remained on earth. The planet continued to tumble toward the sun's gravity.

Following a period of time, it seemed the sun began circling the earth as light periodically came in all windows. The sun seemed to be circling earth in free fall. Distant stars began moving, most in straight lines, to unnumbered of places in the cosmos where they instantly were extinguished. Some seemed to turn somewhat as though being pulled by some force before they disappeared.

Still, millions of kilometers away and approaching its sun, the earth exploded, producing a fireball appearing as large as the sun.

It seemed the place of disappearance were black holes, places we still did not understand. All the lights of our Milky Way, one by one, were going out. Our sun could still be seen even though it was now but a very small yellowish light. A short time later, it disappeared as all the rest had before it.

Following what seemed only hours, nothing existed. The cosmos was empty; all the lights were gone. As well, Apollyon was no longer to be found.

After a considerable time, there came light. It was a hint of promise throughout the empty cosmos. Its color was a soft, soft ultra-light periwinkle blue, resembling moonlight, but as clear as crystal. It had no source and left no shadow. From nowhere, an image began to materialize. It appeared to be a square or cube-like object in nature.

In my mind, I understood it to be 2,414 kilometers cubed. The light gently increased, further defining the outline of the image. I was carried to the interior where at its center was a room, semi-spherical in shape.

I estimated it to be 1.6 kilometers by 1.6 kilometers by 1.6 kilometers high. In its center was a twelve-layered platform, each platform square, was one meter smaller and 1 meter higher than the previous.

The base platform seemed about one hundred meters square. Its construction, gold, silver, and palladium encrusted with gems. Atop was a throne, which no mortal words could describe. The light radiating from the throne increased to that of 600 trillion quasars, illuminating the cosmos throughout.

Drawing closer were thousands upon thousands of people, similar to my state.

Seated upon the throne was one, wearing a blazing white upon white mantle. It was Theotes for whom all creation had waited so long to see.

I was home... I was home!

Third Place

Just Let It Go

by Shannon McKinney

Why do some insist on displaying the Confederate flag? They uphold it as a symbol of the lives lost in a war or a way to honor their ancestors that fought for the Confederacy in the Civil War. Were lives lost for a glorious cause or were they lost because wealthy owners of large plantations wanted free labor?

Plantation owners wanted to enslave a race for financial gain. Many of the soldiers were just poor southerners. In a moment of weakness, good people can get dragged by emotion into bad situations. A comparison in history would be the rise of the Nazis in Germany. Many young Germans were sucked in by Hitler's hatred of the Jewish people, a hatred that rose from envy and resentment. How many young German soldiers would have envisioned themselves sitting on the side of a pit with a rifle in hand as they waited to shoot Jewish men, women, and children when they were herded into the pit? Or would they have volunteered to oversee a gas chamber in a concentration camp?

Today, do the German people fly the Nazi flag to honor their ancestors who died defending it? Did they erect statues of Hitler, Eichmann, or the infamous Dr. Mengele? Most want to forget, make amends, and move on.

The United States is one country. We need to celebrate by flying one flag. Let go of the Confederacy and the slavery it stood for, and let go of the Confederate flag. Let go of hatred and racism. Let go of the divisive past and strive for a better future that builds on tolerance, love, and equality. Just let go!

Short Stories

Liturgy of the Forsaken

by John William McMullen

From a busy downtown corner coffee shop, two seminarians, Justin and Maddox, made their way to Saint Edmund's Saturday evening Mass. As the two men walked through the dank street blemished by urban blight, they approached a seemingly unrestrained dark eyed, thick-lashed, large-lipped, eighteen- or nineteen-year-old brunette girl leaning against a storefront. Her grey trench coat was unbuttoned enough to reveal a red and black dress that betrayed her breasts and her direct stare her intentions. Maddox passed closest to her. She made an inaudible comment with a sigh of exasperation.

Several doorways down, a swarthy woman of shrouded years wearing a dark sock cap and over-sized brown parka sat slumped on the crumbling concrete steps of a dilapidated and boarded up storefront, an apocalyptic shadow of the vibrant young woman. Her head turned at the sound of the men's approach, and she met their gaze; the whites of her smoky eyes were streaked red with life's sorrows.

In the street, an old man collected cans while another explored a dumpster for treasure; around the corner, several more men were huddled against a storefront covered in assorted blankets and cardboard boxes, and for warmth, they were burning forsaken factory palettes in a rusty fifty-five-gallon drum. The icy wind and blanched wintry sky threatened sleet and snow.

Downtown were the icons of modernity: four-star restaurants and cocktail lounges; symmetrically perfect high-rise office buildings encased in tinted glass, elevating high the cultural values of business, cathedrals of commercialism.

Finally, Justin and Maddox crossed the street to the one-hundred-twenty-year-old red brick gothic structure with seven pious concrete statues peering down from their respective niches. The steeples reached heavenward, though now dwarfed by bank buildings and corporate towers; the church doors stood open, the light from within seemingly flooding the street with grace and beckoning all to enter.

The two had arrived at St. Edmund's early in order to spend time in adoration before the Blessed Sacrament, but their evening plans for prayer were altered as they climbed the stairs to enter the church. A miscellaneous collection of tousled and tossed people untidily adorned the crumbling steps: shabbily dressed panhandlers and homeless cadgers clothed in unraveling gloves, twice-bought shoes, and cast-off hand-me-downs from secondhand shops or charity drop-boxes.

As Justin observed their clothes, castoff shoes, and gritty, grimy appearances, he became self-conscious of his own cashmere coat and matching scarf, fur-lined deerskin gloves, and cashmere beret. Justin blushed at Maddox's comfortable Italian blonde wool overcoat and tweed driver's cap and leather gloves. The indigent men goggled the two seminarians.

One man was wearing two different shoes, a pair of discarded polyester trousers from the seventies, and under a lint-ridden black sock cap held out a begrimed palm in their direction. The stranger's eyes, though wide, never met those of his benefactor, slowly rolling back and forth in the bottom of their sockets, never looking further than his own nose.

Justin smelled the man's breath before ever a word was heard from his pathetic petition for "just enough money for a cup of coffee." The supplication evoked a response. Justin reached in his pocket and felt for the change he had received at the coffee shop; his fingers fumbled the silver beads of his rosary as he grasped at the loose coins. The glow from the open church doors illumined the man's outstretched alms-longing hand, smeared and stained fingers, and blackened fingernails.

Justin dropped two quarters, a dime, a nickel, and three pennies in the man's hand. The man expressed his gratitude with a simple nod of the head and a half whispered, "God bless you." Maddox took Justin by the arm, ushering him up the steps and through the church doors.

Upon entering the weathered church, a familiar musty odor and scent of burning candles, lingering incense, vintage pews, and aging hardwood floors greeted them like old friends. As the two made their way past the holy water font, they crossed themselves and walked the main aisle to find a pew close to the sanctuary.

The smell of tobacco, whiskey, and sweat permeated the back of the church where the last three rows of pews were occupied with the dejected, dispirited, and demoralized that had staggered in with hopes of finding warmth and charity. The thought of making a friend or encountering the god whose house it was they were in now rarely, if ever, crossed these men's minds.

The tabernacle light burned brightly, keeping sentry over the sanctuary while the flickering candles from the window sills revealed a writhing body of forsaken believers on the floor and in the pews; the spacious and warm church afforded these abandoned children some comfort. Several dark eyes met his. A gangly black man dressed in sweat pants and a plaid jacket observed Justin and Maddox's every move. Some of the other people clutched their few belongings as if the two meant to abscond with them. An old man, wrapped in an effeminate scarf and a corduroy winter coat, wore mismatched argyle socks, rotten brown dress shoes, a torn Chicago Cubs t-shirt, and olive-green polyester pants as he noisily slumbered in a pew.

The seminarians reverently made their way toward the front of the church. Justin genuflected to the tabernacle and entered the pew; Maddox followed. As the liturgy progressed, Justin became aware of the Savior's words from the gospel: *Whatsoever you do to the least of these that you do unto me.*

At the consecration, the priest lifted high the host. The chant culminated in the Lord's Prayer. As Justin rose to receive the Eucharist, his thoughts turned to the outcast.

After Mass, the evening vespers began. The organ reverberated through the church, the melody blocking out every other noise. The chanting choir of Latin and English hymns and psalms lifted the soul heavenward. At the moment of Benediction, the priest genuflected reverently to the curtained tabernacle and opened the gilded door to reveal the holy of holies. The priest removed the glass *luna* containing the Eucharistic presence of the Lord and placed it in the golden monstrance standing on the altar and knelt in adoration. The congregation mirrored his gesture.

While the familiar chant of *Pange lingua* filled the nave, the priest stood, and one of the altar servers brought him the gold incenser. He raised its lid along the chain and placed several scoops of incense upon the fiery coals. The smoke rolled out of the thurible and filled the sanctuary; the sweet smell brought with it many fond memories of Justin's childhood and growing up Catholic.

The priest then returned the incenser to the server and ascended the steps of the altar again and silently raised the monstrance toward those assembled, and in tracing the form of a cross in the air, he blessed the worshipers with the Sacrament. He then turned to the tabernacle and returned the Lord to his rest. After a brief silence, he turned to the congregation, motioning for them to stand. The service concluded with the hymn *Holy God, We Praise Thy Name*.

Maddox turned to Justin and said, "Let's go, I'm starving."

The two put on their scarves and coats, genuflected, and walked down the main aisle. Justin looked in his wallet as he began looking for the destitute homeless, but there were none to be seen. He asked one of the ushers where the poor people were.

"Who?" a heavy-set man wearing slacks and a sweater vest replied.

"The poor people that were here before Mass," Justin explained.

"Them moochers?" the usher asked. "Hell, they only come around at Mass time to panhandle. I ran them out. This is a church not a homeless shelter!"

"But where are they?"

"I don't know. We had them removed. They were distracting people from worship."

Justin pondered their absence. He should have given them something earlier when he had the chance.

Maddox turned to Justin. "C'mon, let's go."

Justin had come to offer a few moments of prayer to the Lord and realized that in the faces of these, his brothers and sisters, the eyes of Christ stared back at him. As he dipped his hand in the holy water font and blessed himself, he departed the church like a specter in the night. In the three-block trek, he looked intently for the poor people he had seen on the way to church, but the streets were strangely deserted.

"What's with you, Justin?" Maddox asked as he unlocked the passenger door of his Lexus.

"Oh, nothing. It's just those homeless people back at the church."

"Yeah, well, it's not like you haven't seen them before," Maddox said as he pulled away from the curb. "Now, where shall we dine?"

Justin's mind wandered as Maddox mouthed off a list of the best restaurants.

Maddox parked the car in front of a downtown hotel. Justin got out and stepped under the royal red canvas awning, and Maddox handed the keys to the parking lot attendant. Soon, they were escorted to a leather booth with a linen tablecloth, cloth napkins, and crystal water and wine glasses.

The prophetic words of one of Justin's priest-professors resounded in his mind: "*The fashionably dressed and well-fed dine sumptuously while deaf to the dirge of the destitute and eyeless to the garish glare of the street gutters.*"

Justin gave his menu a cursory glance as the words of his professor returned. *"The poor are dying from the apathy of the educated elite, hungering in the heart, thirsting for love, and a just and generous meal of compassion."*

His musings dissolved with the waitress' supplication: "Merlot or Pinot Grigio?"

Unearthing

by Joshua Britton

Tom's elbows dig into the grass when he leans back to catch his breath from retching. Across the yard is the hole. *It deserves another look*, he thinks. Eventually, he'll crawl back over and glance down.

This isn't Tom's backyard; it's Amber's. She's been openly jealous of her neighbors' landscaping skills. Amber's front yard is small and has a gigantic century-old tree smack-dab in the middle, and its fat protruding roots make it difficult to plant grass, let alone a few bushes. There is an equally large deciduous tree behind the house, but the backyard is bigger, and Tom selected a patch of lawn far enough away from the tree where he figured three equidistant holes could be dug for three identical bushes that, once grown in, will not only be a cosmetic improvement but will obscure the rotting fence dividing Amber's yard from her neighbor's.

But, while digging his first hole, Tom struck something hard. He assumed it was just a rogue, water-seeking root, and he hacked away.

Now, he reaches into the hole, picks out a clump of clay, and brushes off dirt to confirm what he thought he saw before: a human head.

More gagging. More dry heaves. Until now, his biggest worry was how to tell his parents he's gotten his girlfriend pregnant.

"There's a dead body in the backyard!" Tom says into the phone. "I was doing yard work, and I dug it up! You need to send someone over quick!"

9-1-1 asks follow-up questions, and he answers: "I found it just now." "I think a man, not sure." "About two feet deep." "Months. Maybe years, I don't know!" "No, I don't recognize him!" "With a shovel. I might've damaged it. Like, cut it." "Please hurry!" "What do you mean you'll try?! Somebody is dead! Please get over here as soon as possible!" "Tomorrow?! What are you talking about? Today! Someone needs to come over today!"

"You haven't turned on a television recently, sir, have you?" the operator says.

"No. Why?"

"There's been a school shooting today. All of our officers are on hand at the school."

"Oh no," – *Amber is a high school teacher!* – "which school?"

"Central." A momentary sigh of relief; Amber teaches at North. "Turn on the TV, sir, and we'll get an officer out to you when we can."

Tom obeys. All of the news channels are covering the Central shooting. So far, three students and a teacher are known to be dead. The authorities assume more, though they haven't yet entered the building; the shooters are thought to still be inside. Dozens of students are unaccounted for, but whether they've become hostages or simply ran off without telling anyone is unknown.

Tom looks out the window. He'd spent several hours online, and several more at The Home Depot, to settle on three self-sufficient arborvitaes that wouldn't die if he or Amber forget to take care of them. His landscaping project, which *seemed* like a great idea, probably isn't going to happen now, even after the excavation.

Back at his hole, and the modest dirt pile next to it, he covers his mouth at the sight of the head, but he's gained more control of his gag reflex in the last few minutes. The shrubs lean against the fence. His shovel lays flat on the ground. As unappetizing an idea as it may be, the more of the body he exposes now, the quicker it will be gone once the proper authorities arrive. He won't try to remove it, only to uncover the rest. He picks up his shovel.

"What are you doing?!"

"Amber, don't come over here!" Tom says. He drops his shovel and rushes to her side. "There's a dead body buried there."

"No, I mean, why are you digging?"

"I was going to plant those for you," he says, pointing at the arborvitaes. "As a surprise. But there's a dead person, Amber. A man, I think. Hopefully, the police will be here soon. I just called them."

"You did what?!"

Amber turns around and rushes into the house. Tom quickly follows. He'd left the TV on, and he glances at footage of police and SWAT ready to bust into the school.

"Where are you going?" Tom calls after her. *She didn't seem that interested in the body*, he thinks. "Why are you home so early?"

"All the schools shut down because of the shooting," she says. She tosses clothes into a suitcase she's pulled out of the closet. "You called the police, you say?"

"Yes, but they're busy at Central."

"Still," she says, "they know." She zips up her suitcase and stands it upright. "Do you have any cash?"

Tom nods toward his wallet on the bed stand. He has a lot of cash, Amber is pleased to discover, and she takes it all.

"I need to leave," she says. Tom is speechless. She kisses him. "I'm so sorry."

* * *

When Tom was a teenager, he figured out that his oldest uncle was born only four months after his grandparents got married. He confronted his mother about this startling revelation, but she excused his grandparents by saying, "They loved each other a little too much."

– Mom, Dad, I'm going to be a father.

– Oh, well, Son, that's ok; these things happen. So, when do I get to meet my future daughter-in-law?

For weeks, Tom has been thinking of little else. He should be grateful for so big a distraction.

When Amber told him that they were pregnant, she listed abortion among their options. Tom was conflicted. He was against abortion, at least that's what his church always told him to believe. On the other hand, how much simpler life would be right now if there wasn't a baby on its way. Turned out, he didn't have a say; Amber was humoring him and had already decided to keep it.

"Let's get married!" Tom said. Just because the baby was conceived illegitimately doesn't mean it has to be born illegitimately. And besides, he thought he wanted to marry her, anyway.

"You're sweet, but no."

"You don't want to marry me?"

"Maybe. But if I do, it won't be because of this."

Tom's grandparents married before they turned twenty. His parents married during college. Tom is the middle child of seven, the only one not yet hitched, and the only one without children of his own. He'd let all this slip early on, and Amber correctly inferred that her new boyfriend was desperate for a wife. She'd had no intention to *re*marry, or at least not so soon. When she did involuntarily imagine happily growing old with Tom, she got annoyed with herself. To preemptively stave off his pressuring, she turned the tables and pressured him into bed. Tom had been committed to preserving his virginity until marriage, but she wore him down. Amber knew that in Tom's eyes this was one of the major perks of marriage, and now he had it without the legal commitment. Now, all talks of marriage could be shelved. It worked remarkably well, until it backfired.

Seventeen confirmed dead: two teachers and fifteen students. This isn't the worst school shooting of all time, but it's up there. The school has been searched once and is being searched again, but mostly everyone has accepted that somehow the killers, now identified, have gotten away. With the suspects at large, nobody will sleep well tonight. Over a thousand students and two hundred employees, the police can't possibly protect everyone.

The networks broadcast pictures of the deceased. Tom doesn't recognize any of them. Amber works at a different school, but he wonders, anyway, if she knew either murdered teacher. Overall, though, his mind is elsewhere, and he watches the coverage with less horror than he did past mass shootings.

Where is she? he wonders. *Where did she take our baby? What happened to the guy in the backyard?* Sooner or later, he'll have to explain to his parents that not only has he gotten his girlfriend pregnant – a girlfriend they haven't even met yet! – but that the baby will almost definitely be born a bastard. Suddenly, that doesn't seem so bad compared to this new scenario:

– Mom, Dad, your next grandchild will be born in prison…

"I made a mistake!" he blurts. "It's not a human body. It's a dog. I didn't look very closely, and I overreacted. But I've double checked, and it's definitely a dog. The police don't need to come anymore."

"Okay, sir. Noted."

– My girlfriend's dog died a couple of years ago. This was before we started going out. She told me it was buried in the backyard, but I forgot.

That's believable, Tom convinces himself. *That's what I'll say if they follow up.*

He makes another call, but Amber's cell vibrates on the end table next to him. Tom hits "end", frustrated that she left her phone behind.

In the backyard, Tom takes another look inside his hole. He's been to funerals, but this is the least healthy corpse he's ever seen. He takes his shovel and dumps in enough dirt to re-cover the body. For the next step, Tom waits for dark.

* * *

Out of respect for the victims of the Central High School shooting, a moment of silence precedes the baseball game. Tom watches from the comfort of his home. Well, Amber's home. Tom still has his apartment, though he's been spending far more than half of his time here, another secret he's kept from his parents.

– I'm almost thirty years old, Mom! I'm flesh and blood. What do you expect from me? How many more failed engagements do I need to go through?

When the time comes, hopefully she'll react better in real life than she does in his imagination.

The networks have shown nothing but coverage of the shooting, even now, during prime time hours. The manhunt continues, and Tom flips between it and the ballgame.

Another catcher's visit to the mound, another pickoff throw to first base, another excruciating seven-pitch walk, the innings crawl by slowly. He pines for the conclusion of this episode of his life, but the game is only halfway through, and outside, it is only dusk.

"You must be Tom."

Tom jumps up from the couch, startled. *Who just walks in uninvited?*

"Who are you? Are you a cop? What are you doing here?"

"You've got guilty written all over you," the intruder says. He walks through the house and out the backdoor, surveys the situation, and comes back inside. "I'm assuming no one's been here yet?"

"Everyone's busy with the shooting," Tom says. "Who are you?"

"Did they give an ETA by any chance?"

Tom doesn't respond.

"Relax, Tom, God. I'm not real thrilled with you digging up the past, but I'm still here to help." Tom feels the urge to wet himself. Sensing his nerves, the visitor offers a handshake. "Derrick, all right? Amber asked me to check things out." Rather than shake the hand, Tom crosses his legs. Derrick gestures toward the bathroom and says, "Go ahead," and Tom scampers off.

By the time Tom finishes relieving himself, Derrick has opened one of Amber's beers and taken Tom's spot on the couch. *Amber has an ex named Derrick,* Tom remembers, though how long ago and to what degree of significance, he's not sure.

"How do you know Amber?"

"I haven't seen her in a couple of years, actually," Derrick says. "Have barely even heard from her, in fact. You see someone every day for a year, and then not at all – it's an interesting phenomenon."

Tom lets this sink in. "Every day?"

"Husbands and wives tend to live together, Tom."

All Tom knows is that he doesn't know anything. He's been in denial about the possibility she might've slept with someone before him. But now, in addition to having impregnated a fugitive out of wedlock who doesn't want to get married, she's a divorcee. His parents are going to throw a fit.

"No one's coming," Tom says. "I called back and said I made a mistake. I said it's a dog."

"Good thinking," Derrick says. "Relax, man." He pats the couch cushion next to him and again offers to shake Tom's hand. "We've got a long night ahead of us. Do you want a beer?"

Tom gives in, sits down, and shakes Derrick's hand. "I don't drink," he says.

* * *

The flashing lights are blinding. Tom has gone through a stop like this before. They'd surrounded a couple of bars and were checking for DUI. Tom was driving through by chance. "I've never drank in my life," he told the uniforms, amused, even proud of himself. He can't honestly say that anymore, though he's still never been drunk. But alcohol isn't the issue, and now he's nervous.

"I've never touched a dead body in my life!" The windows are closed, and he screams inside the car. "It wasn't me!"

– I got my girlfriend pregnant, though. We loved each other a little too much.

At least the arborvitaes are planted. "Amber told me about your idea," Derrick had said. "It's cute. First thing tomorrow morning, though, you're going to want to scour the yard and make sure we didn't miss anything." Two were planted into either end of the expanded and human-sized hole, and a separate hole was dug for the third. They're not symmetrically spaced apart as Tom had planned, but it'll do.

The body didn't lift out in one piece, and Tom threw up, for real this time. What a nightmare, though Derrick didn't seem to be having much fun either.

With its loose limbs folded tightly in a tarp, the body was dropped into the trunk of *his* car, not Derrick's; Tom wasn't given a choice. He's been following Derrick, but Derrick has made it to the other side, and Tom has nowhere to go.

As if the strobing lights on top of the police cars aren't bad enough, a flashlight blasts into his face.

"Have you seen either of these kids?"

The flashlight shines onto the photographs. Tom looks and recognizes the kids as the shooters. "Just on the news," he says. "They're still out there?"

The cop nods and waves Tom along.

Tom exhales and puts the car in drive. The car stalls, and the cop looks annoyed. Tom's face burns. He restarts the engine and pulls through.

Derrick leads him to a secluded farmhouse. Already dug and waiting for them is a hole, behind the barn and next to a woodpile. The two men lift the body out of Tom's trunk and dump it in the hole. Derrick grabs hold of the tarp and yanks it free, like pulling a table cloth out from under dishes. He soaks the remains with lighter fluid and then tosses in a lit lighter. With the body aflame, Derrick throws logs from the woodpile on top.

He takes out his phone. "I think we're good." He listens for a moment. "Sure." He hangs up.

"Was that Amber?" Tom asks.

Derrick nods and gives him permission to leave. "Until next time, Tom," he says.

Derrick doesn't offer to shake hands, nor does Tom say goodbye. He's thrilled to distance himself from Derrick and the farmhouse. He's hurt that Amber didn't ask to talk to him. He doesn't know how to reach her, and he wonders if he'll ever see her again, but then an unfamiliar number flashes on his cell phone screen.

"Derrick says we're in the clear," Amber says.

"Apparently," Tom says. "We."

"I'm sorry about all of this."

"It happens." Tom rolls his eyes at himself, and he's angry at the woman he's hoping to bind himself to forever. "Who was that?"

"Derrick or the other guy?"

"The other guy."

"Do you really want to know?"

He guesses not. "Was he a bad guy at least?"

"The worst."

Tom has the burning desire never to talk about this again.

"Where are you?" he asks.

"In an uncomfortable motel room without a car. Will you come pick me up?"

* * *

Tom's headlights blind two bums leaning against the side of a dumpster when he pulls into the parking lot. "Sorry," he says. He's recently been blinded by a police flashlight, and he knows from experience that it's not much fun.

Amber steps out of her motel room into the chilly pre-dawn air and wraps her arms around Tom's middle.

"Thanks for coming," she says, her suitcase at her side.

"Do you want to meet my parents this weekend?"

"Okay," she says. "And you need to meet mine. Maybe we can talk about planning for a wedding."

"Really?!" Suddenly this has become one of Tom's better days.

Amber likes Tom, there's no denying. Derrick had been a mistake; he'd admit it, too, if asked. She agreed to go out with Tom, because he was safe. But Tom's not only a nice guy who treats her well; she's grown to love him. She's not any good at being a rebel, and today, he's really come through. As much as she tried to fight it, the pregnancy made marriage seem inevitable. But now, why prolong the inevitable?

Tomorrow is going to be a good day, Tom thinks. He'll call in sick. All the schools are closed for the rest of the week, so Amber won't work either. They'll sleep in and have breakfast in their underwear. He'll call his parents, the first step toward telling them about the baby. Maybe he'll call his siblings, too, and invite them all to dinner. It'll be like a family reunion! They might all gang up on him, but at least at the end of the evening he'll be able to walk out with Amber.

As they drive to Amber's house, Tom cracks a smile most of the way. They hold hands, which rest on her lap next to her belly. Sometimes, when she doesn't have a shirt on, Tom thinks he can see the beginning of a baby bump.

Tom doesn't know everything, he's aware. Nobody has told him how the body came to be buried in her backyard, or, between Amber and Derrick, who the biggest culprit was. He doesn't *want* to know. He could dig deeper and try to unearth Amber's past, but people who don't know anything are generally happier.

"This is really nice," Amber says, as Tom shows her the upgraded backyard. They are home and the sun is on its way up. "Thank you."

"Your motel room was number 115, right?" Tom asks.

Amber nods. There were two bums loitering in the outskirts of the motel parking lot. Tom is such a charitable guy that after Amber vacated room 115, Tom offered it to the young vagrants.

Amber worries that they'll trash the place and she'll get blamed. Still, it's hard not to admire Tom's devotion to mankind.

Tom pulls out his cell phone and dials three digits.

"Hi, yes, you know the kids from the school shooting? I think they're in a motel room. Let me give you the address."

The Finding of Estelle

by M. Dianne Berry

Koch Photography Studio, circa June 1972

It's the end of a school year, and as office manager of a photography studio, I'm printing senior picture samples for student yearbook orders. The lobby doorbell rings notifying a customer enters. I hear footsteps and am preparing to greet whoever it is. It's only Jim Rideout, my co-worker, walking slowly with a peculiar expression on his face. And unlike his usual visage, Jim's eyes don't wander. He stares straight into mine as if to share startling news — almost like he'd seen a ghost. When I ask what's wrong, silence sustains him until I ask again. Going into detail, which is so unlike him, he describes what he just witnessed at the location where he photo-captures the last of a 75-year-old building.

Jim is our staff photographer commissioned to take pictures of the demolition of the well-known Vendome Hotel, whose structure erected in 1890. Since it's being torn down, the building commission and a local law firm require photo proof and permission for its razing in the event of injury and/or liabilities. It's easy to get interested in the romance of this sad but necessary process flashbacking moments of the past, from the aesthetically ornate entrances to the elegant dining rooms. A bittersweet part of town, history cries for this abandoned structure as the wrecking ball plunges its heart from life. Downtown employees spend their lunchtime watching it topple. Curious shoppers, visitors, and pining elders huddle to share stories. From dance frolics, jewel theft, fires, prankery and narratives of scandal, much is recalled to have happened between its steep foundation and exquisite towers.

The entire process would take at least four months, from bringing down the walls to compressing the surface and lifting up debris. Jim was there to shoot the gradual changes from every angle, rain or shine. He even skipped his breaks to take extras of the event when the truck crew had a day off, was delayed due to bad weather, or broke for lunch.

*****

About 190 years earlier

Around 1782, a brutal battle took place between anxious American explorers and the Shawnee and Miami natives in the center town of what would later become Evansville, Indiana. The majority of tribes left long before this, but it was obvious there were a few groups righteously lingering around their homeland. Decades later, a Virginian movement of settlers blasted up the Ohio River on a flat boat and loved what they saw from the water banks. Though their own land had breathtaking waterfalls and fertile soils for bountiful planting, commercial trade with the west was limited. Indiana's valley landscape intrigued them while other organic characteristics were similarly appealing – the sinking sun against the open sky and the way the waters ebbed from tough winds. It reminded them of Virginia at sunset and the melting dusk where homes, farmlands, and business structures could be built for growing families.

With the geographical advantage of export trade and a local boom in lumber and coal, a new community was materializing. Seekers observed that traffic flow was quicker due to the Ohio River's rapid undercurrents. Such a feature would be useful for cargo carriers which mandate shipping deadlines and passengers seeking a new place to live. (It was a known fact that they hesitated to migrate from the state of Virginia to Indiana any earlier due to the many floods which is one of the reasons founders passed by the future valley town.) Still, the rich soil and sloping ridges that nestled its ancestors were begging to be used for lifetime purposes. They had come to develop the place that would make a favorable area for new settlers from various states and countries. These groups of trekkers merged and developed until the city was officially founded in 1812 by Hugh McGary Jr. Up to then, the first families and their new friends were living in shoddy cabins.

There was a hopeful life for most folks while a series of menacing events was about to take place for certain others. Among those most talked about were two women- a lady claiming to be Catherine Bernard and her assistant aide whose name was not reported. They occupied a roomier structure near the Ohio generously built by volunteers. Catherine, whose Spanish-French ancestry afforded frequent travel with ambition for a new settlement, struggled during the flourish of smallpox and deadly typhoid fever. Records revealed her husband left one day and never returned resulting in a lack of family support, both financial and personal. (Only one journal was kept by a townsman, and there must've been such misery that its sporadic entries were incomplete and obscure.)

By the looks of her possessions, one could tell Catherine came from wealth. There were special furniture pieces and beautiful imported rugs that graced the small house. Huge crates filled with the best threads of that era were stacked in a storage space behind the house. Rumor was that residents assumed there were more items on the way, but, except for a large container saved for a piano, no other shipments came after her husband disappeared.

A small health staff appointed a Doctor Friedman from Massachusetts to serve the city's medical needs. He could tell by Mrs. Bernard's swollen appearance, something was wrong. Attempting to more closely diagnose, he told her that she was a candidate for the fever and needed further attention. Catherine refused to comply and ignored his suggestions. She spoke French, Spanish, and only a little English, so the communication between them was strained from the beginning and reluctant to discuss anything. What could the doctor do for her? She was so different from the other settlers — nonresponsive, even rude. Folks thought she might've had a hearing problem since she wouldn't acknowledge them socially.

Mrs. Bernard was often contrary – critical of her aide's performance. Once, she was seen pushing her out the front door. The aide screamed until Mrs.Bernard let her back in. After a while, they stayed to themselves and would not mingle.

*****

Later that year, mail courier Will Pajowski delivered the message to all occupants that a record-breaking snow storm was about to hit Southwestern Indiana with a frontal warning of freezing rain and ice. They had to prepare for the coming weather. Neighbors helped each other by securing doors and windows, filling crevices and stacking wood for fire and food. Catherine and her helper stubbornly did most of their own preparation, ignoring the town's helping hands.

The journal was very specific about the character of the storm. On its third day of cold rain, temperatures sharply fell into the teens developing inches-thick ice for miles while frozen winds produced heavy snow covering roads and bridges. The six streets proposed for future buildings were blocked between the riverfront and the southeast trails. They beggingly prayed for at least one day without snow to give residents time to make paths for easier access. But days ran into weeks with more snow and ice. Families were getting sick, some stranded and starving since food supply was low and rationed for women and children. Horses and mules were fidgety and squirming in crowded stables while several froze to death. It was devastating. The journal described it as *horrific*.

Then, finally, a sudden warmer front crept through and broke the pattern. It was over. But the damages were almost incalculable, and they expected flooding. It wouldn't be till early spring when land searchers came to recover bodies of those who didn't survive the storm while doctors examined remaining lodgers. Due to the flu epidemic and killer storm, city officials requested an updated census. Most from the area were accounted for in spite of the death toll.

But Catherine Bernard was missing. Her assistant reported that her mistress did not occupy her bed the second morning of the ice storm. Agents assumed she moved without her aide's knowing. Yet facts are skewed. She confessed that Charles Dubois was the husband of this woman, an aristocrat, and she was living under the identity of Catherine Bernard. Stranger yet, they discovered that Catherine was not the name of the missing woman, but the aide's. She was quoted to have agreed to relocate with the notable widow until she was settled in and no longer ill– as long as she'd maintain secrecy. A misnomer would keep her incognito for undisclosed reasons. The content of their cabin was never claimed, although a name was engraved under some of the furniture. *Estelle*. There was no record of the real Dubois revealing her mistress's true name.

Years after the Civil War, there was a haunting rumor about the search for this missing woman. What was her real name? Was she the temperamental and mysterious lady from Virginia who was either sick or knew she was going to have a child and used the Bernard woman to cover her identity? What would she be running from if her husband was missing, too?

*****

1972- *continued*

Jim finishes his report as I post the conversation here:
"We are about to see the last of the Vendome Hotel. I made sure I took shots of whatever was sealed off in the cellar. The hydraulic hammers were ready to finish up. I nearly died when the crane scooped down one more time and pulled up what looked like a silver coffin. The lid must've been loose, because it flipped open. I gasped and covered my mouth as when watching a sci-fi movie and this was the cliff hanger.) I was in for a shock.

"What is it, Jim? Tell me!" I anxiously pleaded. To illustrate what he saw, he picked up my hand and told me not to tense up, to let it droop. I did. Then, he loosely dropped it, allowing my arm to fall into my lap. *What in the world...?* I thought. Jim's eyes bulged.

"There it was. A body. A perfectly preserved woman's corpse. Just like your hand was limber, when the casket tilted, the side of its door flipped open, and her arm dropped out off the side." He described her in remarkable detail. "She was pretty...had a youthful complexion... normal. Her dark hair was neatly pumped up above her forehead... wore a formal white blouse with ruffles around the neck and cuffs—just like the olden days. She looked like a statue, nothing out of place." I wanted to ask a million questions, but Jim wasn't finished. "There's more. What really got to me was there...tucked under her arm, was a tightly wrapped bundle. The crew thought it was a pillow but it wasn't. Nope. It was a baby!"

Jim was stunned. We all were for a long time. What to do about this startling event? Koch Studio staff hardly ever discussed it, but we don't know why. Like most true stories, they cool down, come up for air every now and then, only to be filed away for more current events and photo shoots. Until recently, the whole story melted away as if it never happened. I waited nearly fifty years to report it. Guilty. I had to insert a story of supposition around the mystery.

*****

Who was this woman with a baby? The entombed, buried till recovered from the Vendome Hotel's area at Third & Sycamore Streets in Evansville, Indiana? Was the physical condition that sickened her a pregnancy where both died at its birth? Listed as missing after a catastrophe, where did she reside for the remainder of her life? Who would have buried her?

I've done extensive research to find photos proving that the exhuming happened. Other than a few friends who remember my telling the enchanting story, I'm the only secondhand witness as Jim and the studio owner have passed away. I've researched past newspapers, spoke to realtors, the coroner, police, curators, historical groups, even the grandson of the demolition crew. The staff at Willard Library were so helpful in the research but with no results.

After being discovered, how are remains legally processed to be traced, and where was this woman laid to final rest? What really happened, and how was this hidden so long, between 1840 and 1972? Now we lost her a second time. Until further notice, I am humbled to report this and at least give her the name that was allegedly engraved under the furniture. Estelle. It is French for "Is she". The name is the message. So...is *she?*

Where in the world is Estelle? Do *you* know?

Aunt Salomie's Revenge

by Phil Kline

It wasn't for me that I did these things. No, it was for the honor of my ancestors and the good of those who will follow me that I committed what some would say was a crime. But almost never am I sorry, and usually on the rare occasions when I think of the past at all, I am proud of what I did. So, for posterity, let me tell you this part of my story, and you can be the judge of it all.

I was born in October of 1902. My parents had just settled 160 acres of prairie land in western Oklahoma on Christmas Eve of 1901, having bought a relinquishment from a man who purchased and later refused that parcel at the El Reno auction in July of 1901. It was a wedding present to Mom and Dad worth $1,000 at the time. My father's parents, who lived in what is now an unincorporated settlement called Virginia, Nebraska, had put up the money. But they never did move to Oklahoma with us. Their gravestones, with still legible engravings, stand in a county cemetery just west of that little town in eastern Nebraska.

There were still Cheyenne and Arapaho in western Oklahoma when we settled it, and I made friends with several of their families in the first decade of the 20th century, before most of them moved east onto the land that had been reserved for them in eastern Oklahoma by the Dawes Act.

My parents worked from sunup to sundown to make a home for us in that forbidding landscape, and even now the land and our home are still in the family. My mother grew a huge garden, canned vegetables and fruits, salted pork and raised chickens. Dad bred hogs, raised horses and mules, did blacksmithing work, and rented out his threshing machine and seed cleaner to the farmers and ranchers who lived around us. Little did my parents know that thousands of feet beneath their farm was enough natural gas and oil to make a small fortune for their children and grandchildren in the second half of the 20th century.

And so it was that in the 1970's the first wells were drilled, and the money began to come in. No longer did we have to depend upon a meager existence from farming the stubborn land; now we could afford new cars, air conditioning, and an occasional vacation to far-away places with strange-sounding names.

And my poor husband Ray—well, he was delighted. We could finally afford the things that city people had, and maybe a little extra. But it wasn't to last. Ray was killed when he fell off a roof while helping a neighbor put up a TV antenna.

Well, it wasn't long after Ray's obituary was published that I met Cal. I should have been suspicious, but my grief after losing Ray was so profound that I was an easy mark. Cal came to my door one day; said he was the minister at the local church-of-what's-happening-now. He offered his condolences and said that he wanted to help in any way that he could. He drove me to the county courthouse where I had to go to settle Ray's estate, he drove me to my lawyer's office several times; we had dinners together and even snuggled in front of the TV. I trusted him, and even when he talked me into signing away half of my oil and gas royalties to his brother's "church mission", I trusted him.

It was shortly after I signed away half my mineral royalties that Cal seemed to lose interest in me. My daughter had warned me about him, as had several of my old, old friends. And finally, I got the message, too. I had been snookered.

There was an old Indian, son of an Arapaho medicine man, whose family I had befriended sixty years before, who was a cattle rancher living nearby. He still practiced the old ways, and I went to visit him. He knew about Cal; his sister had run into the man several years previously in a similar situation as mine. Together, the old Arapaho and I hatched a plan.

Weeks after I had last seen Cal, I called him up and told him that I had some more royalties that I would like to sign over to his brother's "mission", and I invited him over for dinner. It was a pleasant dinner, my best cooking ever, and afterward, Cal went to sleep on my couch. Little did he know that I had spiked his coffee with a potion that the old Indian had given me. Soon, Cal became unarousable, and for all intents and purposes, he appeared to be dead—a fugue state induced by the ancient potion that my friend had provided for me.

The ambulance came and they hauled Cal away to the little hospital in Elk City. The coroner, who wasn't even a physician, pronounced Cal dead. Seems Cal's only friend was his so-called brother who was in on the royalty scams himself. His brother couldn't wait to get Cal into the ground, since the brother stood to inherit all of old Cal's money. Two days later, I went to the funeral, dressed all in black like a grieving widow. As the gravedigger lowered the casket into the hole and covered it with dirt, I saw him stop and listen very intently in the direction of the casket, then go on with his work.

Later, I asked him about it. Seems the gravedigger's hearing wasn't so good; he had just come back from Vietnam with the buzz from artillery and exploding ordinance still in his head. He told me that he thought for a moment as he lowered the casket into the ground that he had heard sounds from inside Cal's casket like a voice, begging to be let out. But that was impossible, wasn't it? Cal was already dead.

The Misfits of Seventh Grade
from Astra and Luna

by Wendy Eastman

Astrid was the new kid at St. James Elementary. Her family moved during the early April cold. I would see her sitting alone at the lunch table or outside in the mended hand-me-down coat, a knitted scarf wound around her head and shoulders, alone on the playground bench. Her long reddish-blonde mane covered her face; her head was always down. Worn gloves covered her hands, the tip of her index finger poked through as she wrote in a brown leather notebook. I wanted to talk with her; Astrid was an outcast like me. We were the opposites of our other seventh-grade classmates. In some ways, we were alike, outcasts of the class, no friends to speak of.

Astrid was pretty in an odd way. Her skin was lily-white with high cheekbones; her eyes were bright green, the color of green lollipops. She was lanky, taller than me. My skin is darker, my face rounder, my hair is dark brown, and my eyes are brown, too. My looks are very uninteresting. The teacher said I was smart but mouthy; I didn't take the hurtful remarks of others lightly.

Missy Dalton, the popular girl, once said, "Lenora, you're an only child because your father couldn't stand having another smart mouth, ugly child like you."

Those words cut me deeply. Firing back at her, I said, "I'm an only child because my father was murdered."

They whispered to each other, calling me a liar. They pointed at me and laughed. Their words cut deep, slicing my heart into pieces. I couldn't make them believe the truth. On the lonely road home, I cried. Before the fork in the road, I wiped my tears and blew my nose with a handkerchief. I didn't want my mother to know why I cried. As soon as I came in the door, Mother wanted to know why I was so sad. I made up an excuse.

"My classmates said my head was in the clouds. I was different. No one ever wants me for a friend."

My Grandfather spoke up, "Having your head in the clouds is fine if you know what type of clouds they are, Lenora." He said the others were jealous because I was so smart.

Yes, I admit it, I'm the weird girl, smarter and less pretty than the other girls. I take wicked pleasure in humiliating my classmates with my knowledge and never bat an eye. This time they caught me off guard, never again.

Astrid was different, too quiet. She never spoke unless spoken to. I saw her spelling test when the teacher handed our papers back. I felt sorry for her. This girl ignored the taunts as if she were deaf to their insults; I wouldn't stand for it myself. She needed a friend. Yes, here we were, the two misfits; I had to save her from the mean girls and the bully boys.

The next day, before the school bell rang, I waved at her and said hello. A sliver of a smile and nod of Astrid's head was her acknowledgment of my presence. The school year was coming to an end. Astrid sat in the row to my left. When the teacher passed out graded papers, I could see Astrid always had red marks. I wasn't sure she passed her exams.

My curiosity got the best of me. What was in the all-consuming notebook? She sat every day on the schoolyard bench scribbling away, except when it rained. During free time, girls gossiped about Astrid's hand-me-down clothes, the latest fads, and boyfriends; the boys made paper airplanes or talked about kissing girls. I'd read; Astrid continued to write. No frivolous gossip for me; I read books about the stars and Greek Mythology. Never looking up, Astrid kept writing in an old brown leather notebook.

Today was bright and breezy, with spring flowers and sunshine. At recess, I summoned up all my courage and sidled up to Astrid. "Is this seat taken?" I asked politely. Astrid never looked up at me.

"You want to sit by me?"

My first thought was, *No, I want to stand here and sing the Hallelujah Chorus for you.*

"I wouldn't have asked if I didn't want to sit here."

"You're Lenora, right?"

Has she been under a rock? "Of course, I am silly. I've been in school with you since you came in April. I sit two desks away from you."

Never looking at me, she said, "I'm sorry. My mother says I'm socially awkward. I guess I am."

"No one in our class likes me either because I'm smart. It would be different if I were pretty."

"I don't think so. You have nice eyes." The monotone way she talked didn't match what she said. How would she know? Astrid never looked up.

I looked at the notebook in her lap. *Egyptian hieroglyphs?* "What are you writing about, Astrid? It must be a great adventure."

"No, it's music."

I was stunned. *Music?* "What do you play?"

I saw some emotion from the ordinarily deadpan face for the first time. In sadness, Astrid recounted what transpired in her home.

"I want to play the piano, but I'm not allowed. My older sister plays the piano and hates it. I sat on the piano bench once." She put the book down to demonstrate. "My fingers were placed on the keys for C major. My sister was furious and tried to smash my fingers with the lid." Her hand returned to the pencil and book. "My mother scolded me." There was melancholy in Astrid's voice, but she wouldn't look at me.

In disbelief, I said, "I'm so sorry. But I don't see how you can write music if you've never played."

"I sit in the other room where I can hear my sister, but she can't see me. I memorize the chord sounds and watch her fingers as much as I can. I look at music books when she's gone. I can hear the notes in my head."

Astrid opened the notebook. "For the Meadowlark," which was written above the homemade sheet of music. "It's my first composition." She smiled; I almost fell off the bench. It was the first smile I saw from her, ever.

In class, I chewed on my pencil and pondered how Astrid wrote music without playing it? It would likely sound disjointed and strange.

"Lenora!" I jumped at the teacher's voice. "Stop daydreaming, or I'll have you stay after school."

"I'm sorry, Mrs. McGee." I sat there embarrassed to death. My classmates snickered and laughed at me.

"The question, Lenora, was, what is Jupiter's largest moon?"

When we studied the planets, it wasn't like me to drift off. "Europa followed by Ganymede and-"

She cut me off, "Enough, Lenora. I only asked for one."

Behind me, Stephen kicked my chair; audible taunts came from half the seventh-grade class. Mrs. McGee told everyone to pipe down.

I slid down in my seat, humiliated for the rest of the day. I probably knew more about astronomy than Mrs. McGee. I'd never got into trouble before. I wanted this day to end. When the bell sounded, the teacher reminded us of testing tomorrow, spelling, and the planets.

Astrid waited for me at the bottom of the red brick stairs. Shuffling her feet, "I'm sorry for you. The teacher shouldn't have been so harsh with you."

I just shrugged my shoulders. Then, I heard sing-songy taunts from some of the boys, "Haha, the Brainiac daydreamed in class! Did you think about your boyfriend? Wait! You're too ugly."

"Shut up, Patrick. You don't have a brain cell between your ears!"

Stephen chimed in, "Two retards! Look at them! A dumb one and a stupid one. True love." The boys laughed and punched each other in the arm. I'd had enough; I hit Stephen hard in the stomach. He doubled over in pain and fell to the ground. The other boys were stunned.

"Run, Astrid, hurry. When he gets up, I'll get a beating."

I grabbed her sweater, pulling her along like a rag doll. We ran into the woods.

Distressed, Astrid cried, "Where are you taking me? I need to go home!"

"My safe place; it isn't far."

Through the woods stood a group of unkempt hedges with a tiny opening. I pulled Astrid inside, putting my finger to my lips, "Shhh."

Inside the small clearing stood two makeshift chairs and an old coffee table. Astrid's fingers closed tight around her spelling book and her precious notebook. She looked up to see a patch of blue sky peeking between the trees.

With a whisper of wide-eyed wonder, she said, "How did you find this place?"

I twittered, "I fell into it." Astrid's forehead wrinkled; she didn't understand.

I listened for the boys, then I pronounced, "Running through the woods, I tripped and fell into the bushes. My knees were bruised, and my arms were all scratched up. I brushed myself off," with a sweeping gesture, and I said, "and here we are. Now we're friends. It can be your safe place, too."

Astrid looked disoriented in her silence.

"Are you all right? Do I scare you?"

Quickly, she answered, "Oh, no! I think it's wonderful," she paused, "I'm not sure how to be a friend."

Her response caught me off guard. "Of course you do. You're my friend. We're the isolationists, you know. We stay away from everyone, and everyone stays away from us. Plus, you know my hiding place. Now you have to be my friend."

"Okay, b-b-but I have to get home," she stuttered. "My mother will be cross with me."

I wanted her to stay longer, but she got fidgety, shuffling her feet. I peeked through the bushes and motioned for her to follow. I wasn't sure where she lived, but I walked her to the main road. I went left at the fork in the road, she turned right.

She turned to me, in her monotone voice, she asked, "You live near the ocean?"

"Yes, the beach isn't far from my house."

"I see," was all she said.

I called after her, "See you tomorrow."

Clutching her books tightly to her chest, she turned to wave at me.

My mother had fresh baked biscuits and strawberry jam waiting for me. I opened the side door, and my grandfather called, "What did you learn at school today, Lenora?" This was our usual banter. My mother kissed me on the forehead. I headed to the living room, where he sat in his overstuffed leather chair. Looking over his wire-rimmed spectacles, he awaited my answer; he said, "Well?"

I stood before his chair, looked at the floor, and spoke softly, "I got into some trouble today." Grandfather had a look of shock on his face as he straightened himself. I swallowed hard as I looked at him.

"I was daydreaming and got called out by my teacher. The class laughed at me." He sighed. "And after school, I punched that bully, Stephen, in the stomach. He made fun of me in class and kicked my chair."

"He has bullied you before, but you never hit him. What made you do this now?" He was disappointed in me.

"He made fun of my friend. She started school in April. Her name is Astrid, and she's," I shrugged my shoulders, "different like me. I talked with her today for the first time."

My mother called to us, "Come into the kitchen. The biscuits are getting cold."

On the way to the kitchen, I whispered for him not to tell Mother.

We three sat at the table. Grandfather looked up from his half-eaten biscuit, brushed the crumb out of his white beard, and said, "Your daughter beat up a boy today." I kicked him under the table. He betrayed me!

"You did what?" My mother was appalled.

Glaring at my Grandfather, I said, "It was after school, and I only punched him once in the stomach. He was making fun of me and my new friend, Astrid."

"You have a new friend?" Mother didn't care that I hit someone; she was excited, almost giddy at my new friend, "What's her name?"

"Astrid Innis."

Mother put her elbow on the table! "What is she like?" She sounded like I'd never had a friend before. Huh, I guess I haven't.

"She's," I thought for a moment, trying to put her existence into words, "very musical."

This bit of information excited my mother and grandfather. When I was five, my father wanted me to play the piano. He bought an upright piano for me. My kindergartener-self didn't have the patience to sit still and play "Twinkle, Twinkle, Little Star." I would later regret it. Even though my grandfather had been in the banking business, he played the cello. My mother sang in the church choir. She could play the melody lines of a song but nothing else. The piano was just an object for me to dust. It stood as a painful reminder of my father's death.

"So, she's musical," he said with a twinkle in his eye, "What instrument does she play?"

Now, I'm going to sound like I've lost my mind. My words came out like a deflating balloon, "Astrid doesn't play anything." Grandfather's jaw dropped, a dollop of preserves fell onto his plate. He squinted at me over the top of his glasses.

"Then how do you know she's musical?"

I threw my hands up, "Okay, this is going to sound crazy. Astrid has this notebook full of compositions she's written. She's always writing."

Now they looked at me as if I were making everything up. Grandfather and my mother shot each other glance. I could tell they were ready to send me to the loony bin. I'm not sure if they believe she even existed.

With my arms crossed over my chest and a stern look, I said, "I'm *not* making this up! She says she can hear music in her head. And she lives past the right side of the fork in the road." The other side of the fork was nicknamed Shanty Town; everyone knew poor people lived there.

With a look of remorse, my mother said, "What a shame."

All I knew about Astrid would fit on the head of a pin.

"She has brothers and an older sister, I think. And I know she's Catholic. She crosses herself at lunch. Her sister played piano and won't let Astrid near it. She, like me, has no friends. We're the misfits."

"You are not a misfit, young lady!" bellowed my mother. "You are smarter than anyone your age."

"All thanks to you and Grandfather." I meant it to be a compliment, but I could tell Grandfather was offended. "I didn't mean to sound harsh, Grandfather. You've taught me many things I would never learn from school." I wrapped my arms around his shoulders and hugged him tightly. "And I love you to the moon and back."

"What kind of moon do we have tonight?" He was quizzing me.

"A waxing gibbous moon," I said with confidence.

"That's my girl."

"Your girl needs to study," Mother said to him as he put his dish in the sink.

"Spelling," I grunted, "but also astronomy!"

Grandfather laughed from the living room, "You'll have no trouble in this one."

Loudly, I said, "My Very Eager Mother Just Served Us Nine Pickles." Mother laughed and said I was clever. She quizzed me on my spelling words. I wasn't so smart on this subject. Always ten words, and there's always one I miss. Once, I'd like to get them all right, just once.

"Spell necessary," she said.

I hated the word, too many s's! "N-e-s-s-i-s-a-r-y."

"No, darling, not correct. She handed me a pencil and a piece of paper. I knew what came next.

"Ten times."

"Oh, gosh!"

"That will be fifteen times for the attitude."

My mother meant business.

After dinner, dishes were washed and put away; I had my time. I sat on the terrace, in the big wooden chair, watching the sunset over the ocean. As the stars began to show themselves, the constellations became clear. When I was younger, Grandfather would sit me in his lap in the evening. The first constellation I learned was Virgo, my birth month of September. The waxing gibbous moon looked like an egg in its oval shape.

I wondered if Astrid knew about the stars. After all, her name sounded like Astra in Latin, which means star.

On my way to school, I felt nervous. I prayed all my words would be correct. I hate spelling, but it's necessary, n-e-c-s-s-a-r-y. God, I hope it's right. In the distance, I can see the playground filled with younger children, some jumping rope, boys kicking a soccer ball, and Astrid-erasing something in the brown leather book. I realize just how little I knew about her.

We exchanged greetings. Astrid kept writing in her book.

"Can you stop long enough to talk?" I asked. I thought it to be bad manners for her not to look at me.

"I'm sorry. We have a few minutes before school starts. I wanted to finish something."

My words came out arrogant, "I'm sorry I interrupted. I'm curious, how many brothers and sisters do you have?"

"Six counting me. I'm second from the end, with four brothers and one sister. She's second to the oldest and the meanest. How many siblings do you have?"

"I'm an only child."

Astrid was puzzled, "It must get lonely."

"Not really. My grandfather keeps me company. My mother teaches me how to sew and do household things."

The school bell called everyone to class.

"We can talk later," I said. Astrid said nothing.

The school days seemed like any other, except recess. Trouble followed me. Stephen and his crew hounded me with taunts and threats. Astrid looked up at me in horror. I left her on the bench, not wanting to involve her. The playground monitors were supposed to be watching. They were more interested in gossip.

Then came a sharp pain in my back as I fell forward to the ground. The palms of my hands slid across the gravel, both knees hit the ground, my chin hit, mashing my tongue between my teeth. My body was falling; I couldn't catch myself. The laughing boys dispersed as I rolled over in pain. Astrid held out her hand to pull me up. One of the monitors rushed to ask who did this to me. If I say who it was, they will threaten me forever. The monitor grabbed a wad of tissues from her pocket to hold under my chin. Astrid led me to the nurse's office.

"My god, child, what happened to you?" the nurse exclaimed.

Of course, I lied. "I was running. I guess I just fell over my own feet." Nurse O'Malley told Astrid to return to class as she began to pick the gravel out of the underside of my chin. It was the worst pain I have ever experienced. I could feel the blood running down my neck. On the edge of the table, my legs swung back and forth.

"Hold this gauze on your neck and hold still," she commanded. I gripped the table so tight my knuckle turned white. A trickle of blood rolled down my leg, stopping at my white socks.

"I think you might need stitches."

An emphatic "no" came from me. Nurse O'Malley said she would have to call my mother.

Alarmed, I said, "No! I'll tell her myself." It's policy, she said. I begged her to let me tell Mother. She made no promise. As she wiped the blood from my legs, she stuck bandages on my knees. A wary look came on her face, "Someone pushed you, didn't they?"

My silence betrayed me. I wasn't about to snitch on those boys.

"Tell me," she demanded.

"I fell!"

She cleaned my wounds with alcohol, bandaged my wrist to keep the blood off my paper. "Can you write with that skinned-up hand?"

I said yes; she sent me back to class with a huge bandage under my chin. I prayed she wouldn't call my mother.

As I entered the classroom, there were snickers; Stephen sneered at me. I looked to Astrid for comfort. She just stared at her reading book. The feeling of betrayal washed over me. Astrid didn't look at me.

"Are you okay to finish the day?" asked Mrs. McGee.

"Yes, ma'am." It hurt to talk. The clock above the teacher's desk crawled. I wanted this day to be over. Now, the dreaded spelling test, a Thursday ritual. My writing looked awful; holding my pencil hurt, I don't remember much about the day. Other than the scar, I would wear it the rest of my life and the silence of Astrid.

I made my way down the path home when a voice hollered, "Wait."

Astrid ran to meet me. When she stopped, her eyes were cast down. She moved like a pendulum. "I'm sorry this happened. It partly my fault."

I looked at her, puzzled. Had she been crying?

"I let you down, Lenora. I'm sorry."

"Why didn't you look at me when I came back to the room?"

"I felt ashamed of myself," her voice quivered. "I told you I don't know how to be a friend."

"Yes, you do. You came to apologize; that's what friends do."

Astrid looked down at her ill-fitting shoes. I dropped my books and hugged her. Poor Astrid didn't know what to do. She became stiff as a board. I could tell there was a lack of affection in her family. This pained me; my family was so loving. Astrid needs to see the love in my family. I'd asked my mother if Astrid could spend the night on Saturday.

We walked together to the fork in the road when she said robotically, "I feel a shadow is following us, Lenora."

"Oh, Astrid, no one is there. No one would follow us. My grandfather would hear me holler, and he'd beat the hell out of them."

The look on her face when I said the word hell would stop a clock. "Don't say that word anymore, or you'll go there!" I thought she'd pass out.

"Okay, no more curse words. I promise. I'll stay here and watch until you go down the hill. I'll be sure no one follows you." Sometimes, she's just strange. Besides I can take care of myself.

Poetry

My Black Dahlia Poison Caterpillar

by David L. O'Nan

What I needed is your new lip poison
Overnight in the broad starry folds
A lush for your black dahlia eyes,
As sonnets written to the midnight crescent
Shall turn to meaningless words.

Of fake crystals, and gentle scarlet fainting.
The caterpillar walks up the paper walls
I watch as it becomes weak,
And it sits on the ceiling.
Depressed into asbestos honey
Knowingly it shall never rule as a butterfly.

The tipped arrows dipped in a Nepalese poison
Took my wandering mind to that of a struck animal,
Or some infected star.
Ripped from its plug in the welkin.
I want to be the naked soul in the body-bag

Hitting the rocks from the waterfall.
In one of your DMT chain link fences
A diamond floats in the brook.

Sensible Shoes

by Erin Pennington

He wanted a woman that wore sensible shoes;
that just isn't me.
He wanted someone plain
straight up and down 6 o'clock,
no thrills, no frills, no fun.
He wanted a woman that only wore perfume on special occasions,
someone who never colored her hair,
wore red lipstick, painted her nails, or drank champagne.
He wanted a coupon clipping, sports enthusiast, to offer him daily applause.
He wasn't interested in deep thoughts, long term goals, or dreams;
he didn't want anyone that might rival him.
He got what he wished for,
as he drowns in her puddle.

You, Before

by Jerrica Magill

You make my heart flutter, flitter, prance
around in an endless loop of what is, what
was, and just might be if I'm lucky enough
to be proven wrong and
brave enough not to fear you.

You missed me, you say,
and the way you say it makes me
warm-
like the taste of my mother's apple pie
during the holidays.

You miss me, want me nearby,
want to hear my voice,
want to travel with me,
want to call me "Baby."
Do you mean it?

You call me:
Baby-Darling-Mi amor-Honey-Cariño-Babe.
You tell me I'm the best.
But do you mean it?

My heart still flutters, and
my body is warm, but I shiver...
because I've heard all this before.

Life on Venus

by Jerrica Magill

My love for you is like no other magic
you'll ever encounter,
and I believe that if you suffer
long enough, you'll discover this truth.
My unending love for you.
My love for you is incessant even
when you wish to forget it
and toss it and burn it
to the ground. I left it for you.
My reliable love - so blue.
My love for you is at times aggressive, so
completely obsessive
that in my time most pensive,
I forget it's becoming too possessive and cruel.
My domineering love for you.
My love for you is murderous, violently
teetering, a growing psychosis,
but I know that given the chance, you'll choose us
over them, you'll possess my blue.
My black and blue love for you.
My love for you looks like ashes flicked off
a cigarette then tossed
to the wayside and then lost
in a smolder, a glowing cost of youth.
My evergreen love for you.

I Still Forgive

by Jerrica Magill

I will never get it,
that type of pain and heartbreak
that causes one to dilate
their souls and grind a
friendship served upon a silver platter.
My life matters.
You left me battered.
You ruined me with my name
upon your tongue in vain,
and you think yourself righteously insane
in your malice.
My heart matters.
Yours is tattered
with the reality of loneliness so deep
that you chose to break me.
Thanks for the clarity.
Now, I'm done giving my charity
to false witness-bearing
scars like a fitness medal
for running marathons of serial validation searches
into the eyes of men
who want your thighs more than your lies.
This is by far my worst goodbye.
My goodbye matters
much more than your hello shattered.

Emerald Peaks on My Mind

by Jerrica Magill

Sometimes I miss mountain air.
The breeze chilly,
the scent of lilac.
The breath stays fresh and clear -
     not like here.
I went for an afternoon run.
The air was thick,
the sun shone too hot.
My breath staggered, slipped gear -
     like your leer.
This breath feels a bit unfair.
Like mountain air,
like the beating sun.
Like a girl crying tears
     of false fears.
I don't miss the mountain sun.
The rays sneaky,
sky hazy heat fog.
It singes your skin pink -
     sunburn ink.
I do miss mountain rain.
The drops pinging,
cleansing the air's grime.
It washes the hillside -
     for new strides.

Senseless

by M. Dianne Berry

Careful! They may hate you
once the world shrinks its
sinful morals down your
throat; taste the bitter grief
while burden builds and sinks
afloat and spends what's been earned.

Sweet song in sour notes;
social heat, freeze its growth,
grace for guilt, this for that.
Fools will miss and contradict,
stretch the knee, then genuflect.

Don't use a blistering tongue–
the same one that prays
a wicked spirit weaves the lies
truth or tales, let's not forget,
fall, prostrate, and surrender.

It's come to this? A senseless bore—
Best live this life in metaphor.

Sea of Trees

by M. Grace Bernardin

In the forest
Dark, Alone, Eerie,
Strange creaking noises
Death, decay
All around
Yet in the midst
Sunshine thru the trees
Strange and beautiful insects
And rain, sweet rain
Baptizing the broken
Coming down hard and clean
Healing the open wounds and cuts

Two souls
Trying to find their way
Back to the path
Back to God
All around
Even more present
In this place of death and decay
The Via Dolorosa
Jesus continually stumbling
Simon pressed into service
Reluctantly helping

Crumpled balls of paper
Their trail of breadcrumbs
Yellow winter purgatory
A contradiction
Like life

The coldest, darkest
Most lifeless of seasons
To mix with
The brightest, sunniest
Most hopeful of colors
The two come together and create
The small white blossom
She has passed on

The Voice

by M. Grace Bernardin

It came upon me again last night
A sudden eclipse of darkness in the light
And the voice which whispers there is no choice
As it plants its poison premise
Like a blight

At the table of friendship our sorrows to drown
A glass of wine raised all around
But the voice which whispers there is no choice
Crept into the banquet
And found me without a sound

That's right
A voice without a sound
A spark without a light
A parasite on the ground
Waiting to rise
And enter the unguarded unbound

And so, the guest became the host
My mind, my gut infected most
But the antidote I heard was hope
And love
All open wounds to close

The Third Option (Paralyzed)

by M. Grace Bernardin

When that malevolent shadow blew in on a breeze
It was fight, flight,
Or freeze
It seems you chose the last of these
It cracked your head
You couldn't think straight
It broke your legs
You could no longer ambulate
It broke your spirit
And made you fear it
Stuck
Paralyzed
It made you believe its lies

The paralyzed man
Must be lifted by others
Fathers, Mothers
Sisters, Brothers
Through a hole in the roof
His cot must be lowered
With persistence and faith
This mission is powered
Until finally he lay
At Christ's feet for the healing

With just one word
He regains all his feeling
His soul no longer
Stuck in the sin
His feet no longer numb

He feels again
A surge of energy
Replaces all the lethargy
At the sound of His voice
At last another choice
Rise and walk

My One Last Dream

by M. Grace Bernardin

Driving, always driving
Alone
Down familiar streets
Grey and winding
Through the shabby part of town
Destination
That building on the corner
Or was it the other corner?

Listening to the radio
Singing along
With the declarations of love
That sound in my ears
From the air waves
In melodies
Carved out of electric strings
And calloused fingers
And hearts still hoping
Like mine
Still beating
Imagining the day
When my one last dream
Comes along
And heals the color blindness
In my eyes
Until all the shabby grey
Turns bright with color
Like Vista Vision rainbows
Like the dial on the color TV set
In my parents' basement

It only takes a slight turn
My fingers reach for the dial
In anticipation
The song is over
And my heart
Floats back down
Where it belongs
In my chest
My feet
Back on the ground
A prisoner of gravity

Woods

by M. Grace Bernardin

I was there
Just for a moment
Fully aware

Alive in your time
Where there is no time
Where the past does not haunt
Where the future does not worry
Only the present exists
And we behold it together
Away from the scorching sun
Into the shelter of the woods
The music of the birds
The sunlight streaming
And falling
In uneven patches
Through the dense
Mid-summer greenery
Landing here and there
Wherever it can find an opening
To light up small spaces
On the cluttered woodland floor
I thought I'd lost you
These past few days
Until you called me
Into the woods
To sit on a log
And watch ants
Crawl over dead leaves and sticks
And hear the birds

And marvel
At the slightest breeze
That rustles the leaves
And the patches of sunlight
And the deep green all around
And just waste time
But it's your time
Which is no time
And all of eternity both

I was there
Just for a moment
Fully aware

The Light I Can't Avoid

by M. Grace Bernardin

There's a dancing wavering light
That draws me
Like a moth to a candle
Like a poor, stupid insect
Wretched and doomed
The poor creature struggles
The pulse of a fluttering wing
A faltering thorax
Stuck inside the light fixture
Trapped and tattered
Struggling in vain
To free itself?
No...
To merge with that pretty light
Poor, stupid insect
It doesn't even know it's trapped
Stuck and dying
A prisoner of its own folly

Oh please!
Blow out the candles
Leave the lights out
I'd rather fly in the dark
And bump into an occasional window
With nothing to guide me
In my blindness
But instinct and faith

Beautiful Memory

for Amy

by M. Grace Bernardin

She remembered the dress
It had belonged to her mother
Muted blue silk
Covered in black lace
Out of fashion,
So the mother
Gave it to her little girl
For dress up
For imagining
For childhood play
She put it on
And gave another old cast-off dress
To her friend

They danced together
In the darkened basement
Of her childhood home
To the strings of Tchaikovsky
On an old Victrola
So slow and lush
So melancholy and melodic
So bittersweet
So heartbreakingly beautiful

And they danced
In their dress-up dresses
In the darkened basement

With just enough light
From a small rectangular
Ground level window
Casting just a few rays
Of waning sunlight
Onto a small patch of carpet
And they danced right through it
Ballerinas
And it was magical

Today her tired eyes
Pool with tears
From all the loss
Down through the years
Including the old cast-off gown
And the beloved childhood friend

Walls Fall Down

by Richard Westbrook

The towers are falling, the angels are calling us on
their horns to awaken the beast.
The sun might settle out on the west, but it rises
out here in the east.
We bringing the thunder like Thor and cripple you.
An explosion tells me what the ripple do.
Waves of radiation poisoning
rivers are dyin', and oceans are boiling,
so tell me who's dyin' first.
The top of the list, the elitists of earth,
they pillage and destroy as they please
the primary targets until they leave
to populate Mars somewhere in the stars.
Biblical verses hidden in my bars.
Years of abuse spelled out in my scars.
I don't walk on eggshells for no one.
Go to Hell for what you've done.
Can't tell me to tone it down, cause I been around
long enough to know some
of you dudes don't deserve your fame.
So, here we come to be household names.
2020 we makin' sounds.
Breaking down walls and making towns.

Taking the Trip Back to Innocence

by Tim Heerdink

Some blow out like candles when their time comes
while others may flicker in the hesitant way
a bulb does just moments prior to a twister
tears every fabric & board from the shell
that houses soul with memories & love
until only foundation remains in sight.

First of the senses to be obscured is sight;
nobody is aware of when relief comes.
The one true constant in stress is love
for there can be no alternative way
to emancipate oneself from the shell
than through the eye of the twister.

Within life's untimely destructive twister
we regain the innocence of a child's sight.
Precious peers may not tell by the shell
& its appearance, but a truth comes
in a most undeniable way
when the aged call out for their parents' love.

Through the years a transcendence of love
stronger than any recorded twister
spirals its evolving path in a way
no pupils are needed to witness the sight.
Age does not take away the feeling that comes
upon the touch which releases the shell.

As a reborn child free from death's shell,
no ill will can distract unconditional love

nor produce fear when darkness comes.
Having withstood each hurricane and twister,
a peaking sun's rays are within sight
& it leads to the eternal way.

A parent surrogates the sun this way
when a child shucks their own shell
to open blinded eyes to new sight;
becoming the caregiver out of love
in preparation of the next twister
that, despite the sun, inevitably comes.

Lack of sight clears the way
for what comes out of the shell
is innocent love before the twister.

Wishes for My Last Birthday with You

by Tim Heerdink

Wax sticks stare my direction
in anticipation of a plea
for something I do not have
to appear from nothing
& bring me a smile
on this wonderful day
of turning another year
older & wiser as they say.

I'd like to personify
cancer if you will,
so that I could
penetrate its every
orifice without any
prep or love at all.

Yes, I want to hear
its screams for
mercy that'll never come.

Perhaps cancer may
have a mom I can
get my way with, too.

Seems only fair
since I have to hear
the cries of agony
my mom feels
every day as she slips
further away from me.

I'm thankful to have her
one last time
on my special day.

Too bad wishes
rarely come
to fruition.

I'd take her pain away.

Harmacy

by Tim Heerdink

Burnt out P on the sign overhead,
I see you lookin' my way like,
*Why haven't you made it out
of this maze doctors got you in?*

My fingers are tappin' to the tune
reverberatin' through my box
as my thoughts conjure images
of overdosed friends whose hopes
were to get that easy fix
before tricks of the mind
caused death by suicide.

Those capsules led me to the fire,
held my fingers as they blistered
& burned permanent scars within.

Hypocritical pricks tryin' to make
a buck off the pain their clients feel.

I say clients instead of patients
because they want us to think
we are all sick needing maintenance
when really the cure is of our control.

We pay them to tell us
it'll all be okay
if we learn to swallow
& pay the bill on time.

My dad told a crooked MD
not to give expensive injections
so infectious to another person.

Mom died too young
hoping to clear psoriasis
with this miracle drug.

Now this killer's got the COVID
& another under his wing
with the incurable glioblastoma.

I can only hope his own remedy has the same effect.

Meal of Memory

by Tim Heerdink

Our senses have the ability to trigger memory at any random point
in the day when you least expect a wave of emotion to overtake
you & make a brief stop in movement life calls for in progress.

We have five that work in these ways to transport us through
time and place like an H.G. Wells machine on the map of which
we cannot see nor hold for it is within the depths of our own
minds.

I cut the bread, the texture of the crisp crust opening itself
to a welcoming warmth on the inside as I dig my thumb deep
for the spread makes me think of the one who is gone from here.

Sitting at the table, I am no longer at Gray Brothers
where she used to fill up her tray like a school girl
on break but around family together for celebration.

You spend countless hours breaking bread with those
meant to carry you through life like a bible tucked
between arms with care so as not to fall apart.

Food keeps us breathing like a tune-up of the old machine,
lubricating the organs with good drink & keeping
the tank at just the right amount of full for now.

These flashbacks ignited by the rendezvous
of substance & tongue are always welcomed,
but they never quite satisfy my appetite.

Breach

by Tim Heerdink

Shields up, form a structure
strong enough
that they can't puncture
& take our women
& children.
Did you forget
they always come first?

Hold steady on this
levee, the river
is rushing in.

Some of us won't make it;
we don't all know
how to swim.

Reviews

Review for The Ghosts of Our Words Will be Heroes in Hell by The NÜ PROFITS OF P/O/E/T/I/C DI$CHORD

by Tim Heerdink

Think about what you would get if you had four of the most prolific and talented poets combining their unapologetic honesty into one piece. That is what The NÜ PROFITS OF P/O/E/T/I/C DI$CHORD are about, and their latest collaborative release, The Ghosts of Our Words Will be Heroes in Hell from OAC Books is a perfect sampler of what each individual has to offer.

The poets include Jason Ryberg, Damien Rucci, John Dorsey, and Victor Clevenger. Each has their own style, and yet it all goes together so well.

Ryberg captures the life of a man who both longs for and rejects normalcy the world often tries to push on people. He reflects on a girl he lost his chance with in the past in "Consolation Prize" while looking at how surprising civilized his surroundings are while sitting on his porch in "LA-Z-BOY on the Front Porch". As a touring writer, sometimes you have two realities you would like to have while you are often left in-between or with neither in the end. "Gas Station Famous" sets the scene perfectly for three of the four men as they take a break while on tour.

Rucci paints the struggle of poverty, addiction, and the hard work it takes to get by with poems like "When You're Poor," "But When I Get Clean Baby," and "Most Days". The tug of war between positive and negative forces is present in "Jesus Can Wait". He builds toward what he desires in life by leaving his past self behind while hitting the road to the next chapter.

Dorsey writes pieces about his interesting friends and acquaintances that are often filled with a humorous tone. Tales of 'Crazy Mark' in "The Finger Has Got to Come Off" and "As Curtis Drives By" lighten the mood during his more serious observations while he waits in airports or recollects what his peers have said and done. When one has travelled to many places and seen countless individuals along the path, of course there will be stories. The best drama is the kind that is not your own.

Clevenger pays tribute to his children and to his love while also looking at the country with its politics, starting off with "Poem for My Grandson". He conjures artistic images in describing the harshness of mental illness in "The Color of Deep Depression". There is pain associated with looking back to the past. This literature helps with the coping for both the writer and the reader.

Although these four poets come from different parts of the country, they have come together with the common interest of the art. Words have a way of connecting people even in times where being in the same location is difficult. Man may only live but for a short time, but ideas, poems, and love shall continue long after the last breath.

Midwest Writers Guild of Evansville

Vol. 2

Contributors

M. Grace Bernardin has worked in Human Relations and Pastoral Care and she lives in Evansville, Indiana. She is the author of the novel *Odd Numbers*.

M. Dianne Berry is a Christian woman who's been writing since she was nine. Although internationally published in poetry, she's always adored great stories, true or made up delivered in poignant detail. She is the author of two other books: *McMullan's Cellar*, *Things Happen . . . When Women Dream*, co-author of numerous anthologies while edits and writes reviews for other writers. *Pennywinkles & Mimosa* – a collection of poetry and prose, is now available. Dianne is a wife, mother, and *Nanah* of three grandies, cooks, plays the guitar and is a senior member of the Midwest Writers Guild.

Joshua Britton is a professional trombonist living in Louisville, Kentucky with his wife and two small children. His work has appeared in many journals, including, *The Bombay Review*, *Tethered by Letters*, *Cobalt Review*, and *The Tarantino Chronicles*. He is the author of the short story collection *Tadpoles* and editor of the anthology *The Notes Will Carry Me Home*.

Don Brooks has written five novels, several short stories and poetry since retirement. His genre is Family and History. Every family has a story. It matters little its shape, size or color. It's theirs and deserves to be shared. He certainly has proven it true.

Jake dh is the author of multiple books including two sci-fi-action novels in *The BulletProof Ghost* series and the horror anthology, *Nightmare People and Other Short Horrors*, and the chapbook, *Zoned Out*.

Wendy Eastman is an Indiana gal with a Georgia heart. Her roots are in New Albany, Indiana. Wendy graduated with a B.F.A. in theatre from Wesleyan College in Macon, Georgia. The former US Army photographer left Europe for The Golden Isles of Georgia. Her children grew up on the beaches of Georgia's barrier islands. Her novella, *Torn Pages*, is the conclusion of *Nina's Choice*, her first novel. Her third novel, *Astra and Luna*, will be released in 2022. She also authored the chapbook, *A Wednesday Night Ticket*.

Tim Heerdink is the author of *Final Flight as the Fog Becomes Night, Somniloquy & Trauma in the Knottseau Well, The Human Remains, Red Flag and Other Poems, Razed Monuments, Checking Tickets on Oumaumua, Sailing the Edge of Time, I Hear a Siren's Call, Ghost Map, A Cacophony of Birds in the House of Dread, Tabletop Anxieties & Sweet Decay* (with Tony Brewer), *Welcome Home, Andromeda*, and short stories "The Tithing of Man" and "HEA-VEN2". His poems appear in various journals and anthologies. He is the President of Midwest Writers Guild of Evansville, Indiana.

Philip Kline was in junior high school when he began to write short stories and poetry. That all ended in 1972 when he entered medical school; he was so busy assimilating what others had contributed that he had little time to offer anything original of his own. Now, after 43 years as a physician, Philip has stepped into another role. And with whatever time he has left, he wants to give some knowledge back, with the hope that some might find inspiration in his words.

Jerrica Magill is an ESL and creative writing instructor, author of short fiction and poetry, and dog-mom to a rambunctious Siberian husky. She authored the chapbook, *It Started with Linguine.*

Shannon McKinney is a southern Indiana writer and retired teacher. She is the author of two poetry books, *Apple Skins* and *Blackberry Jam;* a novel, *Fences;* and a collection of short stories, *Emerald Edges.* McKinney, who has also been published in several periodicals, lives with her husband near Winslow, Indiana.

John William McMullen is the author of *Eugene & the Haunted Train Bridge*; *Poor Souls*; *The Miracle of Stalag 8A*; and assorted short stories. He is currently working on a novel. McMullen resides in Evansville, Indiana.

David L O'Nan has been writing & reading poetry for almost 20 years. He has edited/contributed to "The Fevers of the Mind Poetry Digest", and also curated an anthology book "Avalanches in Poetry " writings & art inspired by Leonard Cohen. He has poetry books of his own found on Amazon. His work can be seen on feversofthemind.wordpress.com and on Twitter @DavidLONan1, as well in poetry zines such as Royal Rose, Elephants Never, Headline Poetry and Press, Voices for the Cure (an ALS anthology) and more. He has read poetry throughout Mid to Southern Indiana, Kentucky, and New Orleans, LA.

Erin Pennington is a 2010 graduate of McKendree University and a 1994 graduate of Eastern Illinois University. She possesses a Master's Degree in Educational Leadership and a Bachelor's Degree in Secondary Education English. She has been an educator since 1994. Ms. Pennington is from Benton, Illinois, but has been a resident of Carmi, Illinois since 2000. She is the author of *Something to Say.*

Richard Westbrook (also known as King Kold) is a poet, musician, and the CEO of the record label, Power Requires Hustle. His albums include: the *Drink at Rich's* series, *Drink Alone*, *Down the Rabbit Hole*, and *2020 Family Reunion*.